"Self-confidence is knowing who ___ your God-given i___
Oluwatoni A___

"Self-confidence is carelessness. No emotions _____ back from doing anything you desire. No boundaries limiting you".
Sokari Rufus ♛

"Self-confidence is being able to be you with no obstacles. It's feeling like you are enough and it's knowing who you are"
Camille Cabral ♛

"Self-confidence is being humble in the sense that instead of thinking less of yourself you think of yourself less.
Bertheli Dawson ♛

"Self-confidence is the ability to openly display a strong, positive attitude towards yourself"
Esther Erogbo Denedo ♛

"Self Confidence is being able to understand that you're not perfect but still loving yourself and presenting that love to the world"
Anulourun Ojo ♛

TABLE OF CONTENTS

Prologue 3

Introduction 13

Chapter 1: Birth 16

Chapter 2: Anew 24

Chapter 3: Sacrafice 43

Chapter 4: Kindred 75

Chapter 5: Eloquence 83

Chapter 6: Teenager 91

Chapter 7: Blockage 109

Chapter 8: Admiral 123

Chapter 9: Letter 1 138

Chapter 10: Letter 2 145

Prologue

"Valerie! Come and help me in the kitchen," I replied in exasperation.

Countless times, I was interrupted by the beckoning of my mother, interrupting my writing. I would usually be writing poems, and stories, or glued face-deep into my diary. I kept my works hidden of course; such creative thinking was forbidden in my household.

I can recall the one time I was caught in the act of writing. It was a Friday evening, and showers of misery poured down relentlessly outside. I assumed the sound of the rain would distract my parents in some way, or at least give me enough time to do some extra writing. They were downstairs, and I was in my room. My father was placed on the sofa, watching television, and my mother was occupying the kitchen (as per usual). She was preparing my father's meal when she summoned me from the top of her lungs.

"Valerie!"

"Valerie!"

"Valerie!"

After no response, she turned toward my father in a psychological agreement, and my father flounced upstairs. I was so lost in writing in my diary that I couldn't even hear my father's footsteps approaching me. The words I wrote in my diary mainly consisted of what I had completed during the day and how I felt; there was not much a seven-year-old could write at the time.

"What are you doing? Can't you hear your mother?"

The deafening silence swarmed across my room. I was speechless. It took a few seconds for my father to realize what I was doing, and then he erupted like a volcano. He bolted towards my writing and tore it up into smithereens. I cried uncontrollably. My tears suffocated me, making it intolerable to breathe. The tears flowing down my cheeks weren't of anger towards my father but rather that I felt a part of me was missing. I felt stripped away from my identity. There was a connection between me and my writing, so when it was torn, I was also torn, physically and emotionally.

This pain was only added to as, with the help of my mother, I was hit with a wooden spoon three times on my left wrist, forceful and accurate. Later that night, when my father was asleep, my mother counselled me and urged me to divert my attention toward the housework and that my writing was a distraction from my duties.

After that, I was never caught writing. All of my writings were under maximum surveillance. Writing was only completed when I was either home alone or when I was certain that I would not be caught. Regardless of the circumstances, I had to make sure everything in the house was attended to cleaning the kitchen, and the bathroom, and preparing food. The kitchen was most likely the most visited room in the house, even more than my bedroom at times. I wasn't going out with my friends or 'hanging out,' but rather, I was visually learning recipes my mother cooked.

By the time I was 18, I had learned everything there was to know about being a good wife. All the meals I had prepared over the years were muscle memory, second nature. Like most girls my age, I only had two options: enrol in training to become a teacher or marry into a family where my sole obligation relied on my husband. I wanted neither. I wanted to learn how to write and make a living out of it.

My friends and I all decided to go into training. My chances were already slim of becoming a teacher; I was one of the few coloured in my neighbourhood. I always felt inferior to my friends. I never really felt I belonged, simply different in all aspects. My nose and lips were abnormally grander than their counterparts. What I called "friends" were not necessarily deserving of that title. They were more like people I associated with and interacted with to fill the void of emptiness inside. They made me feel like an outsider, queer. My braided hair did not compare to the angelic flowing strands of beauty they owned. Boys weren't interested in me, especially the ones that shared the same reclusiveness. Initially, I thought that if we shared an identical appearance, then it would correlate with the level of interest we had for each other. However, my complexion deterred guys. They assumed I would be loud and aggressive, and they wanted someone who was more calm and friendly. This made no sense to me because I was neither of the stereotypes, they had placed on me. But, as time passed, I realized that someone was always going to be prettier than me, someone was always going to be smarter and funnier than me. This was beyond my control. The only thing I had any control over was the perception of the person in the mirror.

"Coloured women don't get no jobs." I heard this phrase repeatedly as if it were on repeat. Unbothered by this, I decided to go into training. Teaching was never my intention. Writing has always had a place in my heart. Money made from teaching was only going to be a stepping stone to fund my writing. That was the plan. At the time, I had already written four drafted novels that I was proud of; I only needed help to publish them.

During this period, my love for writing reached its peak. Writing always gave me the ability to express myself in ways I felt were silenced. It allowed me to rearrange reality when I didn't want to live in the one I resided in. It was a coping mechanism for everything that occurred in my life. I knew I could be successful, but all I needed was the money.

Within a couple of years, I was an established teacher in my local community. I worked my way up from being a supply teacher to one of the most respected teachers in the school. I was able to work consistent hours with a decent wage. I was able to do things that many of my other peers were incapable of doing. I had a small house, a second-hand car, and most importantly, my independence. I had the freedom to do what I wanted, while my peers were still restricted under the monitoring of their parents' roof. From an outside lens, I defied the odds. I exceeded what others thought I was incapable of doing.

During this time, I met a kind-hearted and genuine man. We first met at our local cafe, a place I used to go for a change of environment to read and write. The cafe unlocked new forms of creativity for me, more than just sitting at my desk in my small room. Mondays and Thursdays, were the days I went, and without a doubt, he was always there. Returning from work, he would order the usual: a croissant with jam in the middle along with a hot chocolate. It was strange to me why he always ordered this, especially during this timeframe, but I never built up the courage to ask him.

Weeks went by, and all I could ever do was stare at

him; this was the only form of interaction we shared apart from the odd nod of approval if I were lucky. This scenario occurred for the next couple of months until one Thursday, while I was sitting at a desk reading, he approached me.

"What are you reading there?"

"A poem, Chainsaw versus the Pampas grass."

"What is it about?"

"Man's violent battle with nature," I responded.

"Who wins?" he asked eagerly.

"Nature, of course," I replied.

"Nature always comes out on top," I added.

"Why would they fight in the first place?"

"Territorial, I would guess, perhaps to see who holds more dominance."

"That's dumb."

"How is it dumb?"

"They should learn to value each other's differences and accept each other's strengths."

"And what strengths might that be?"

"Well... the chainsaw is misunderstood, repressing his feelings through violence, but deep down is innately protective."

"And the pampas grass?"

"The pampas grass just needs to be appreciated for its elegant, colourful beauty."

"So, you're saying they should work together?"

"Exactly, they should help each other."

"What's your name?"

"Osiris, and you?"

"Valerie."

"It's lovely to meet you, Valerie."

"Likewise," I replied.

Our conversation on the poem extended for a couple of days after that. Days turned into weeks, and weeks turned into months. We weren't even talking about poetry at that point. We found every reason to go to that cafe and every reason to meet each other. When months quickly turned into a year, he proposed, and we were married shortly after.

At age 24, I had everything I could ever dream of. I had a stable job, and a loving husband, but one thing was still missing: a hole in my life that I still felt needed filling. It was a feeling that felt like I was limiting myself in some way like I had more to offer, more than being a teacher. It was never my intended plan, something just used to fund future projects. I had already surfaced just enough to start full-time, so I decided to quit my job and try to push my passion into practicality.

When I quit my job, many people thought it was a mistake. They said that I could have just been doing it on the side. However, I knew it was a rational decision. If I was going to be a successful writer, it was going to take all my time, more time than I was accustomed to allocating. I had to put everything into it.

In line with my expectations, things were progressing as I had imagined. With the help of other writers, I developed relationships where we were able to read and exchange our works with each other. I received a great deal of help from this, as it gave me the tools to reach the point where I was able to publish my first piece of work. My life was finally becoming the culmination of all the thoughts I had as a child. I was seeing them unfold in my reality. I could feel myself reaching new leaps creatively, but like with most things that I experienced, I was hit with a break. I was pregnant, unexpected and stunned. I wasn't ready for a baby, at least not at this moment, but it was something I had to accept.

With not gain much success from my first piece of work, I was advised by my husband to re-apply for another teaching role. He thought that we needed to have a stable income to provide for our new child. I listened. Eight months into my pregnancy, and I hadn't even picked up a pen; my dreams of what I wanted my life to look like swiftly drifted away. I made the conscious decision to postpone my dream and direct my attention elsewhere: to my awaited daughter.

Introduction

DEAR BASKETBALL,

Many of my teammates and coaches supported me tremendously through my decision to depart from the game of basketball. Despite the support from the people around me, I must admit that I was sceptical during this time. I've never done anything else in my life. I was accustomed to such a rigorous pattern, that I couldn't imagine myself leaving it.

Basketball was my life. I put myself under mental and physical stress because of it: eating, sleeping, and dreaming basketball, and now that it was over, I had no clue what I was going to do.

Once retired, my time was spent at home, doing nothing. My only source of purpose was dropping my kids off at school and when that was completed, I spent hours motionless on the couch. I was incapable of finding a substitute to occupy my time. I kept having a voice in my head asking, "What now?", and for the first time in my life, I didn't know the answer to that question. It was an uncommon feeling for me. Until this point, I always had a sense of comfort, reassurance almost, that I had a specific goal in mind that I chased. My career always allowed me to strive for new objectives, but now... there was nothing to chase, nothing to work towards.

I attempted to go into different industries, but I was not experienced nor interested enough to manoeuvre through those types of environments. The words of my mother however savoured me during this, perhaps the only thing I needed to progress through this stage of my life. She would always tell me "Do what you love", and I never fully understood what she meant until now. I realised that I was never going to love anything more than I did for Basketball. I derived happiness from it, even when I wasn't playing.

From then on, I knew what I wanted to do. I decided to be a coach, and I have been coaching ever since. On reflection on the years of playing and coaching, I wanted to take the time to show gratitude towards you. You have given me joy that is incomprehensible to even measure. You have opened so many doors to not only me but to everyone around me.

I want to explain all of my feelings to you in this letter in the only way I know how. I envision this as a blank canvas on which I paint all of the distinct colours and patterns that have influenced my life up until this point. This is my life's work of art, which you have contributed to. You along with another special individual have helped me create a beautiful picture. I never did get in touch with that person; he just seemed to disappear as things got better, but

more details of that will be given later. But let me remind you of where it all started and how I fell in love with you...

Chapter 1

BIRTH

The moment my mother entered the hospital, she was in an unimaginable state of pain. Every bone in her body was screaming immensely, crying out for help, wishing for this torture (me) to stop. She sang a sweet song named "AHHHHH" continuously throughout her journey to reach the hospital. As a result, her tonsils began to ache, only adding to the pile of pain she was already experiencing. Her limbs were unrepairable, and it seemed that her pain further grew as time moved forward. The pain was her new friend now and for the rest of the night. It was never going to leave her until I arrived, which was still uncertain at this point.

Time was also moving slowly, at least in my mother's eyes. For her, everything was in slow motion: the car was like she was on a first-class trip on a snail that made regular pit stops, and my father's decision-making was like someone had put a pause button on him every time he concluded, traffic lights were like adverts playing on television, only an obstacle to this never-ending race, and other cars appeared to be overtaking her on purpose, just to disrupt and slow her down. Even though there was no traffic, my mother saw the vehicle only move an inch, she was blinded by time. Time was doing her no favour. Minutes felt like months, hours felt like years, days... this day, this day felt like centuries to her.

My father had driven at a tremendous speed to arrive at the hospital, despite time taking a slow brisk walk from the perspective of my mother. In his eyes, he was driving at a death-threatening pace, skipping cars, and avoiding traffic. He was decisive, making quick and sharp decisions: doing several things at once and still being able to counsel my mother during this time. Traffic lights were not an issue: he had gone through five of them, the majority of them being red. He went past bins, drove on pavements, and I'm pretty sure he ran over somebody (but he would never say so).

That night, both of my parents faced a similar challenge: time was not on their side. Time seemed to be chasing after my father. It was all happening so fast that he couldn't even take a breath of acknowledgement that he was having me. That thought was in his head, but only in the back of his mind because he had other things on his mind. He had to think about my mother and everything that entailed: her anguish, her screams, and her vulnerability. He had to make certain that both she and I arrived at the hospital safely and in one piece.

When he successfully reached the hospital, he felt a fraction of relief off his shoulders, at least for him, the fate of my birth wasn't his responsibility anymore: it was the hospital. However, this relief was short-lasted and proven to cause more stress not only to my father but to my already struggling mother. The cause of their added stress was the variety of patients that they were met with in the waiting room. It intimidated both of them as they thought they wouldn't be prioritized. Each patient was ranging with different illnesses and struggles that varied in severity but still needed attending to. A few patients were adopted with no more than a bruise on the knee, something that seemed insignificant to the elderly patients whose lives seemed to be slipping away after every unbearable cough they were experiencing.

You could hear the lack of immunity in the room with coughs, sneezes, and the occasional vomiting, increasing in volume as they all waited impatiently. These sounds were synchronized with agitation and multiplied into frustration as well. These feelings were further strengthened by the fact that my parents also shared in these feelings of urgency, as they too wanted to be attended to. As both of my parents dwelled in the waiting room, their feelings differed: my mother, in excruciating pain that would be immeasurable for me to even describe, and my father, growing in anxiousness as seconds passed.

My mother gazed hopelessly at my father, "I… don't… want… a repeat of last time," she said sobbingly as she looked away quickly to shed a tear. "Stop," my father interrupted. "Don't speak negatively, everything will be fine," he reassured her as he took her hand. Their hands were held tightly together, as they continuously waited in oneness for the attention of the medical team to come to them. On the outside, my father offered my mother a sense of control and security, but on the inside, he may have been even more fearful. He didn't believe the words he said to my mother, why would he? He couldn't control my fate, nor could he control how healthy I would be, I was only in the hands of the hospital. All he could do was wait alongside my mother comfort her and appear less worried than she was.

Observing from afar, my father appeared to be seated next to my mother with a sense of uneasiness. The entirety of his body reflected a state of discomfort. His wrinkled forehead, right down to the pores in the soles of his feet, sweat shivered like a snake. It is probably due to the puissant winds he experienced when he was speeding in his car, that he found his hair untidy and chaotic. His back was leaned forward, his elbows were positioned at an uneven angle placed on his unparalleled thighs. His fingers were in a locked manner and resembled the shape of a fist below his chin. On the collar of his shirt, there was a trail of moist sweat running down from his wrists. His shirt was already in perspiration and stuck to his back like dense glue. There was a corresponding rhythm in the tapping of his left shoe and the pace of my mother's heartbeat. Their discomforts were shortly put to an end. They were accompanied by a worker in the hospital to the emergency room. When they arrived at the room, they were met by two individuals: one male and one female (at least what I have been told). The female was black, and the male was white. Both individuals were clothed in the same leon-blue attire. Both were wearing masks that covered a substantial proportion of their face to where only their eyes were visible. The material that withheld their footsteps was almost identical. They were both of parallel identities.

Before both individuals had the opportunity to introduce themselves, my father insisted that the male individual was to operate on the procedures of my birth. The female may have taken offence to this, but it was apparent that she was only a nurse, and her purpose only served to assist the male operator.

For the next couple of hours of my mother being in labour, the doctors proclaimed my stubbornness to enter the world. My "unwillingness to cooperate" only served to bring more pain to my mother. While this occurred, my father trapped himself in the corner of the room, biting his fingers incessantly. He was too scared to be anywhere near my mother; he did not want to bring any bad luck.

Relief soon touched the hearts of everyone in that room, as eventually I was born. "It's a boy," "Thank God," my father exclaimed. Moments after my birth, I was moved into another room, where I would be cleaned and covered with a blanket while my parents waited.

"What would you like to name him?" the Doctor questioned.

"Seraunin," my parents replied in unity.

"Are you sure?"

"Yes, we are sure," my parents replied in unity once more.

"Quite a peculiar name for a child like that," the Doctor stated. He then went to the other room along with the nurse to gather documents.

Chapter 2

ANEW

As I grew older, my love for basketball grew with me. As I began to comprehend words and phrases spoken by my parents, understanding their instructions, as I began to know what was right and wrong in my parents' eyes, as I began uttering sounds that led to pronounce words and phrases, as I began maturing as years passed, one thing became clear: my love never changed.

You would find me at the age of just four throwing my unclean socks into the spacious laundry basket repeatedly, trying to model my favourite player's form. At that age, I would not have been described as a typical child. I didn't want to be around other infants my age. They simply did not strike me as relatable. I didn't feel a connection to them. I only wanted to spend my time on one thing. It is unusual to discover your passion soon after birth; some people spend their entire lives searching for it.

Some people never find it at all. I was fortunate to discover what I wanted to do with the rest of my life, and I wasn't going to let anyone or anything stop me from pursuing it. Besides my ambition, my parents had other ideas. I was reaching the age when it was time for me to attend school. For me, school has always been an institution, a system put in place to limit your creativity in what you want to do in life. I believe they distract you with tests to only enhance your anxiety and place assessments and homework to pass the time: valuable time I could be using to practice. The school was not going to teach me to become a better basketball player. I was going to be stuck stagnant in a cycle of something I could not escape from. However, I had no choice. I needed to go to school, not just by my parents, but it was the law, a law that every 5-year-old had to unwillingly abide by; I was no exception. When it was finally time for me to attend school, it gave my parents a sense of relief, but I cannot say my feelings were reflected. For them, I would not be disturbing their sleep with my deafening playfulness. Until that point, I was rarely without a basketball. Instead of eating or sleeping like my peers, I was focused on improving my basketball skills.

To put it mildly, I would have been described as a vibrant child, the kind of vibrance that my teachers would now experience. School was a new environment for me, a dissimilar experience that I was not used to. Anxiety had replaced excitement as my new neighbour. My parents' feelings differed, however; it was something they looked forward to. At least for them, it was now the opportunity for them to see me interact with kids my age which they tried vigorously to attempt before this time came. I didn't see the idea of interacting with my peers as an opportunity, but rather a construct that I was forced to experience. I was going to be thrown into a wildfire for which I had to adapt and make my way around or be burnt alive. It felt like this fire could not be put out the more my mind occupied the thoughts of interaction and socializing. It only fueled as the days began to get closer.

This reached its peak the day before school commenced. I had never felt this way before. It was the first time in my life that basketball did not fill the entirety of my thoughts. Even the small sections of the day where basketball did, it didn't give me the level of peace that it always did. Basketball was always able to uplift my spirits, but it seemed that the thought of entering school kept me restless physically but mentally drained. Throughout the day, my parents seemed far more enthusiastic about school than I did; it was as if they were looking forward to going to school while I was dreading every moment of it. They constantly reassured me that "Everything will be alright," but this did not offer me comfort as I am sure they intended to. Nothing could have calmed me down and made me feel better at that point unless you suddenly announced that school had been cancelled and I no longer had to go. It was hopeless. When my parents woke me up that morning, I was beyond fatigued. I did not get any sleep, of course; I was employed in the thought of associating myself with my other classmates the whole night. My parents did not seem to care though; they were ensuring that I was on time so that they would not be late for work. I obeyed their command unwillingly and sped up my preparation to get ready for school. As any other day, I had my breakfast: cereal with one slice of toast. I had no appetite, however, so it was a struggle for me to finish my meal. If not for my parent's impatience, I would have taken the whole morning to finish my breakfast. By the time I finished my meal, I was practically dragged to the car, for which I experienced my most anxious journey. I observed that the level of terror grew as we got closer to the school.

The ride to school could not have been much shorter, even though it was only a 30-minute car ride. As we got closer, I felt as though I had less breath in my lungs. By the time we arrived at the school's entrance, my heart had completely stopped. I got out of the car, and panic struck me right away. Trepidation. With each step I took from that point onwards towards the school, my legs began to tremble uncontrollably. I lost all motion and feeling in my legs. I could not walk in a distinct pattern. Each stride was unbalanced, and it felt like everyone was glaring at me with their judgmental eyes. I was farewelled by my parents, but this still did not give me any comfort in the situation. I had no clarity on how I was going to be able to manoeuvre my way through this environment. It was like I was a small fish in a sea full of sharks.

Before I had time to speculate on my fears, the bell rang, and I was directed to my class by an older student who made an accurate assumption that I was lost. Suspiciously, I followed his lead, and we arrived at the class. I was then greeted by my new teacher, who shared the same qualities as the older peer, perhaps the whole class shared this same quality, a common classification that excluded me.

"Good morning class, my name is Mrs White."

"Good morning Mrs. White," responded the whole class as I looked wondrously into space.

"What's your name?", Mrs. White asked curiously.

"Seraunin."

"Well...Say-wrong-ying, when I say Good morning you say it back, do you understand?"

"Yes."

The whole class, including the teacher, shared a moment of laughter at my naivety to the conventional greeting. Shortly after, our first task was assigned to us. Each of us was asked to write on a piece of paper, which our teacher had ripped roughly from her desk, what we wanted to be when we were older. From a left toright landscape order, I wrote proudly that I wanted to be a famous basketball player. After each student had written what they wanted, the teacher collected the pieces of dreams and aspirations one by one. While she read them on her desk, we waited silently and patiently.

"Who wrote that they wanted to be a famous basketball player," the teacher exclaimed with a slight chuckle. I raised my hand boldly, hoping that I was going to receive some level of praise in front of the whole class, but I got the opposite.

"A person of your shaded exterior will never have any form of recognition to become famous. How do you expect to be advertised with the way you look? You need to aim for something within your reach."

The whole room joined in an alliance of laughter toward the situation. I, too, joined in the laughter, but I did not understand the joke. I did not understand the humour of pursuing a career as a professional athlete. I later found out that I wasn't the only student who put an athlete-oriented future on my piece of paper, but I seemed to be the only student singled out.

Proceeding from the performance of laughter and humiliation, it was time for a break. Each of us was aligned one after the other in the canteen waiting for our dreadful meal: three pieces of broccoli, a shrivelled portion of mashed potatoes, supported by baked beans and coated spontaneously by cold gravy. This meal was accompanied by a minuscule carton of either strawberry or vanilla milkshake. After I was served last (a decision made by Mrs White), I tried to locate a seat, but there was no space for me. It seemed like the whole class had separated into different groups like everyone had a designated seat that I was not told about. I decided to sit by a stall next to the exit so I could be the first one out when it was time to go to our next lesson: enduring the pain of my nauseating meal until the break was finished. Eventually, when the bell rang, we went to our next class.

"Good morning class, my name is Mr. Pale."

"Good morning Mr. Pale," united the whole class, including me. After this interaction, Mr. Pale wrote on the board in white chalk: "Linguistics 101."

I and my classmates were put through a variety of tasks for which we had to sound and pronounce different words and phrases. I appeared to be the only one struggling with the reforms of pronunciation. I couldn't voice out certain words that other students were pronouncing. I was singled out and humiliated for the second time, and it was only my first day of school. I didn't know it was possible to embarrass yourself with such magnitude in one day. After class, it was time to go home, a sense of relief for me. I had noticed my dad waiting from the corner of my window, and I couldn't have been more alleviated to see him.

"How was school, Son?"

"It was Okay."

This was the only form of dialogue that passed through this 32-minute, 47-second journey. Reaching home, I rapidly sprinted towards my basketball and spent the remainder of the day with it. This was how I spent most days while I was in school. It was a never-ending cycle that didn't stop. My wish was to spend more time playing basketball, but I was stuck in a trap of school, a nightmare that I had to relive every day.

The concept of school was not something I was very fond of. It stole 8 hours away from Basketball. I needed to improve as a player, and school was hindering me from that. School as an institution never offered me a sense of comfort, the social construct of it gave me uneasiness. The daily interactions between people made me uncomfortable. Everything about it did not seem to give me a false sense of security. School is meant to offer reliability, and a second home, but all the school ever did for me was give me a lack of reassurance. I was most vulnerable at school. I felt most threatened at school. I didn't feel safe as it promoted itself to be. I felt like an ant: a missing puzzle piece out of a horrifying picture. Desolate. I was not capable of the notion of 'making friends'. I was incapable of even glancing at the people around me. Fear was installed into my DNA. Afraid of confrontation, I ate alone during lunchtime.

I was only ever comfortable with what I knew best: basketball. Basketball was my only ever friend. The only friend I ever needed in my life. A companion that was loyal to me and would not judge me. It did not care how I looked. It did not care about my appearance. It did not care whether or not I was nice to them the day before. All it required of me was my time for which I was willing to give all of it. There, of course, were individuals who attempted to be friendly towards me, but I was not keen towards the idea. I didn't trust them; I felt like they had ulterior motives. Their true intentions hid behind their smiles and laughter.

When I wasn't lost in my thoughts of isolation and disparity, I would frequently use the limited time allotted to me to practice. During break times, I would work on moves that I had practised the night before. Only during this period in school would I feel rational. My training schedule would change depending on the weaknesses I thought I needed to work on.

While I was practising, individuals would ask to play with me; I would often say yes only with the condition that I was able to verse them. This at least offered me the chance to use the moves that I frequently and tirelessly practised. This was one of the rare moments where I shared physical trading with someone apart from the hugs my mother gave me. However, this physical training was short-lived, as I often disincentivized my peers to train with me as, in their words, I was "taking this too seriously." I did not comprehend these words at the time as the concept of playing basketball for fun didn't make sense to me. From what I have seen, Basketball is meant to be played competitively between opposing players, and the feeling of victory and triumph is what both players strive for subconsciously. The feelings associated with victory should make you feel accomplished and that is considered 'fun,' at least to me of course. I would watch basketball legends be surrounded by praise and accomplishment when they won, either individual accomplishments or a team victory, but their spirits were maximized in euphoria. I wanted to chase that feeling, and that is why I practised so relentlessly, so I was put in the best position at any point in my life to experience that feeling.

Despite my acceptance to train with my peers, my behaviour toward individuals started to spread across the school like wildfire, and I was now labelled as 'the weird kid.' Students across the school would treat me differently when I would pass by. It made me feel isolated and deprived of a chance to re-label the rumours about me. This impression of me would stay for the rest of my duration through school, and there was nothing I could do about it; it was out of my control. I could not change their minds or give a different impression to them; their opinion of me was permanent. What did I do wrong? What was wrong with me for them to make those accusations? These questions affected me in ways that I couldn't understand.

As a result of this, when I was not occupied playing basketball, I would curl myself like a scrunched piece of paper in the empty area within the school I could find. During this time, I would sit with my thoughts and reflect on my behaviours during the day. I would ask questions; How else could I have acted in this interaction? How was I perceived when this or that occurred? Who was looking at me and what were they thinking about me when I did this? Apart from these questions, I would, of course, be drowned in my own emotions and resentment of the school. Each day felt as if time was moving in slow motion, and I was the only one experiencing it.

When I was in classrooms, it felt like time stopped as a whole, I would spend the majority of the time glaring at the clock located in the top-right above the teacher's desk. Classwork, like some students, did not occupy my mind, but rather the duration of my departure from the class did. I would have been viewed at the time as academically unmotivated, at least that was what my teachers exclaimed. It is not like I could not learn, or I was "thick" as my peers would say, I was only just willing to learn and grow intellectually on one thing.

There was a wide range of groups that occupied the classrooms: there were the 'nerds' who inhabited the front of the classroom and would usually answer all the questions the teacher would ask. They never missed a deadline and were always punctual. Towards the middle section of the class lived the 'casual students'. Although I was towards the bottom half of the middle section, I would have classified myself as a 'casual student'. I was not disruptive to the class to the point of excluding the learning of the front section of the classroom, but I also was not engaged enough or showed 'enthusiasm' to the lesson to obtain intellectual status among my peers.

Feelings of boredom or excitement always seemed to circulate across my classrooms varying on the engagement and participation of each student. However, this collective feeling did not seem to come past me. The contrasting emotions touched everyone apart from me, leaving me isolated yet again. Desolate. The feelings that did seem to designate with me were feelings of vulnerability. This was not because of my lack of interactions with my peers but because I felt robbed. Robbed of my time. I felt that I could be utilizing my allocated 24 hours elsewhere, rather than learning about 'photosynthesis' or 'algebra'.

The school was filling me with all these distractions to slow down my passion. It was like it pressed a pause button on my ambition and pressed play on my route to failure. All school did for me was offer self-doubt as the less time I spent away from the game of basketball the more lack of trust I had in myself to fulfill my goals. For all I know there could be someone my age who was working harder than me and potentially with more physical gifts than me. These were the thoughts that occupied my mind during the classroom.

I always felt picked on by my teachers, they would often ask me questions that they knew I did not know the answer to, and they wanted to single me out in front of the whole class. It's not like I gave them a reason to do this, other candidates suited well for the position of humiliation. Some students would disrupt the classroom while I tried my best to stay unnoticed. I strived to not be peripheral to my teachers, but I still seemed to be picked on and put in the spotlight amongst my peers. Most students like attention, and in some way, I did too, but this was not the type of attention that I wanted. This attention was the type that I wanted no part of.

If I ever were going to gain attention I would have rather preferred gaining attention for my efforts in basketball, at least that way it was attention I would feel comfortable around and attention I deserved. Up until that point, I had never gained recognition or praise for playing basketball, there had always been negative opinions towards my admiration of the game of basketball: from my peers to my teachers and my father.

As the teacher made efforts to pass knowledge onto my enclosed brain, pointless thoughts continued to occupy my mind. Days were long, and strenuous, and seemed to be stealing valuable time away from me playing basketball. That was all I ever wanted to do. It was all I was ever willing to give time to. I didn't really have friends, I isolated myself in big crowds. It was overwhelming and uncomfortable, so I did not participate in the term "socializing".

There was rarely a moment where I was not thinking about basketball. Basketball was my life. It dictated my day-to-day interactions as well as my emotions. You could always tell when I was in a good mood, it would usually be right after playing. It enticed me in such a way that I was willing to give all my time to it. My parents again thought otherwise. They thought it would be good for me to try new hobbies to occupy my time with. They tried to make me play instruments and gain other skills that I could potentially use when I was older, but I was never engaged with it. I signed up for Karate at age 3 but according to my mother, I cried the whole time I was there. Not because I was hurt or injured but rather because I was not in an environment that I was comfortable in, there was only one environment that I ever wanted to be in.

My Karate teacher said I was stubborn, undisciplined, and unenthusiastic. These adjectives are not usually associated with 3-year-olds, but I wasn't the ordinary 3-year-old. My constant crying lasted for around a week until it became a detriment to the other children who were having fun and to the parents who were supporting their children. This failure didn't stop my parents from trying to put me in other things though, as within that same month they put me through dancing lessons. The result was the same. Constant crying infused with nagging done the job, and within two days I was kindly asked to never come back.

You would have thought my parents would have given up by then, but they always used to say "We want to put you through a range of different activities and skills so that when you're older you are not limited". Although now this makes sense to me, back then I could not comprehend why my parents would go to such lengths to put me away from basketball.

When I was around seven, my parents tried again to get me involved in various hobbies and activities, but this time they thought they could go down the musical route because I always got excited when any song related to basketball came on. But, like with most things they tried, a basketball ended up in my hands.

Chapter 3

SACRAFICE

For my ninth birthday, I maintained my enthusiasm for the game of basketball. My parents presented me with a large collective gift. I couldn't figure it out, and the birthday wrap covering the gift didn't give it away.

"Happy Birthday Son," they both stated in unison as they both waited for me to open the gift. Impatiently, I ripped the wrapping paper, in the hopes of discovering what could occupy such a large exterior. Once I vigorously ripped all the wrapping paper from this gigantic box, I was met with the letters *"Adjustable Basketball Hoop."* I was beyond ecstatic, speechless almost. I bolted towards my parents and gave them the biggest hug I could physically conjure. I held them tightly, squeezing their bodies together, then released them as quickly as I could so that I could open the box.

My father helped me assemble the hoop in my garden, while I gazed in disbelief that I received this gift. He put screws and bolts precisely where they needed to be put in and adjusted the hoop to a suitable height so that I wouldn't struggle using it. I insisted that he adjusted it to the regulated height of ten feet, to replicate what the professionals played on. I wanted to be like them one day, and being used to the same height they played would be a start.

Once the basketball hoop was assembled, I can't remember a time when it wasn't in the same position that it stood in. I took good care of it and made it precious, it was the only gift I would utilize from my parents until I turned the age of 18: the only present that I truly valued and cherished.

Once I received the gift, every day after school I would work on my layups with my right hand until I mastered it and then I would switch to my left hand. Once that was enhanced, I would try different variations of finishes with my right hand to challenge myself. Some layups were awkward in terms of timing and foot placement, but the key for me was to make myself uncomfortable and challenge myself to get better. Once this was completed, I would execute this again with my left hand, ensuring that there was a balance in terms of skill with both hands. Sometimes I would even prioritize time, especially for my left hand just to ensure that it had no flaws so it would not be exploited when the time came for me to use it. I would often watch professionals play and what separated the goods from the greats was the crispiness of their fundamentals, especially with their left. I made it imperative to make my "weak hand" a strength.

Once I had mastered finishing, I moved on to shooting. I tried to mimic the form of Kobe Bryant but obviously, my arms were not strong enough. Restlessly, I would practice form shots to ensure that my shot mechanics remained the same after every shot. Once that was completed, I would move a little further out ensuring that I perfected every shot. I would not advance further out until I heard that swish sound at least 25 times in a row. The volume of my shots increased as I got stronger because it enabled me to shoot more with quantity and quality. Once stationary shots from all areas of the court were in my arsenal, I would advance to free throws. I worked tirelessly on my free throws: getting to the point where one day, while practicing, I made 102 consecutive free throws in a row. I had to make sure this was my biggest strength as it was the only shot in basketball that did not change for anyone. I made them as challenging as possible: ensuring that when a game did come, it would be muscle memory and something I was not stressed over or even worried about.

Once this skill was perfected over time, I would create different scenarios of shooting that I thought I would experience in a game. My knowledge was limited though; I could only go off what I saw in games played by professionals. I would shoot with speed, range, off-balance shots, shots off the dribble, and all types of shots that were imaginable. This gave me a sense of security as in any situation where I could potentially be put in a game, I was prepared to not only take the shot but make it as well.

Once shooting became a strength of mine, I moved on to passing, pretending the wall was a teammate and passing to the wall in various forms with both hands. My inspiration came from professional point guards. I admired their creativity and ability to make a pass out of any inconvenient situation. The only limit to practising passing is that it requires the involvement of another person to truly replicate the experience in a game. Although my interactions with my peers were limited, when they did ask to play me 1vs1, I would let them score so I was given the chance to pass them the ball but in a way that I was not comfortable performing. This was a way for me to also work on my game without the opponent realizing. Me letting my opponents score was rare though because I had also mastered my defense both perimeter and interior. I would watch a variety of defenders at their craft and watch their tendencies as well as their skill as well. I would watch their facial expression when they committed a foul and their reaction to that foul, but also their reaction when they had a block or a steal and see how they responded to that. From this, naturally, my IQ for the game enhanced.

To progress further I would look at the finer details when I was watching a basketball game. I looked at the strategies the coaches would implement based on the last play. How the defence was able to capitalize based on the mistakes of the offensive player. What mistakes were made on the offensive and defensive side, why they were made and whose fault was it that those mistakes were made? I enjoyed this side of basketball because it felt like chess in terms of strategies and how reactive each play is based on the previous play. All of this contributed to my smartness for the game, especially for my age. If only we were tested on Basketball in school, I would have gotten all As.

Amongst all these skills that I developed over time, the only thing that stayed consistent was my ball handling. I once read an old article on Pete Maravich that he developed good ball handling because basketball was an extension of his life. I stayed true to that quote as I cannot remember a time when I was not dribbling a basketball. It became a part of my lifestyle. Even my walk reflected the number of dribbles I took with a basketball.

This was how I trained to become better over the years. I perfected these skills, constantly trying to figure out new drills and ways to make it challenging for myself. I made situations and scenarios uncomfortable while I was practicing making sure not to stay content, especially when I felt I was improving. I always wanted to make sure my persistence to get better stayed stagnant. I grew creatively because of it as well, I came up with different angles on the backboard I could use and different spins and rotations on the backboard that I could explore. I first started using the white-squared line located just above the rim, but I soon found out that it wasn't the only way to make consistent lay-ups. If I was able to use different locations of the backboard, then I wouldn't be predictable. High off the backboard would be difficult for taller defenders to reach, a spin-off of the backboard may prove difficult for the opposing defender to pin.

This was the type of thinking that occupied my mind while I was practising. I always enjoyed new ways of testing myself: mentally and physically. I found a thrill in examining my ability through different drills. I enjoyed seeing where my strengths would be limited as well as seeing where my weaknesses (a lot during that time) would hinder my growth. It was a never-ending quest that I travelled through. I enjoyed the obstacles and difficulties on the way to get to my preferred location, as I knew arriving at the destination would be sweeter. I knew the destination was not going to be smooth; it was never going to be, and I would never appreciate it that way.

The next day arrived, and I was met with a change. An unbalanced to the accustomed lifestyle I was used to. It was a new teacher, a science teacher, one that seemed more relatable. I could spot his indifference before he ever spoke a word that day.

"Good morning, class."

"Good morning, Sir."

"My name is Mr. Brun, and I will be starting off this term by teaching Neurology. This first lesson I will be encompassing the importance of sleep." The whole class, including myself, shared an area of confusion. We couldn't comprehend why we would be learning such a thing in the environment of a school.

Mr. Brun spotted the collective confusion and proceeded to ask the whole class, "How many hours of sleep do you get?"

"I get 7 hours," one student shouted out.

"I get 10 hours," another shouted proudly.

"I get 9 hours," another remarked.

A variety of answers kept constantly pouring out of the classroom, some on the greater end of 12 hours and others on the lower end of 6 hours. As each answer was shouted out more and more, I became singled out. Eventually, it reached a point where I was the only one who did not contribute their answer, and this seemed apparent to the whole class. I expected as usual for this to proceed in public humiliation from my teacher, but I was met with a different approach.

Mr. Brun softly spoke, "How many hours of sleep do you get young man?"

"I get around 2 hours, sir."

The whole class gasped in shock.

"What are you doing if you are not sleeping?" Mr Brun asked concerningly.

"I am training," I replied.

"Training for what?"

"Basketball."

"Interesting," Mr. Brun replied. He then took a few seconds of silence.

"Do you realize you could be a better Basketball Player by sleeping more?"

"How so?" I responded eagerly.

"A lack of sleep dictates your sympathetic nervous system. In simple words, not sleeping enough gives your brain unrest. A lack of rest for your brain blocks the pathway of recollection."

"What does that mean?"

"It means all the moves you practice and work on will be difficult to remember and transfer onto muscle memory."

"What does that mean?"

"It means all the moves you practice and work on will be difficult to remember and transfer onto muscle memory. My eyes expanded in disbelief when he said those words.

"Not to talk of the benefits to your nervous system. You'll experience an enhancement in your extracellular serotonin levels. If you are in a better mood, you're less likely to feel anxiety."

"I wasn't aware," I stated in disbelief.

"Many aren't," Mr. Brun replied. "If everyone knew the value of sleep, we would all be much healthier and stressless individuals."

The remainder of the class was spent with each of us writing about the benefits of sleep. I had learned more in that singular class than in all my previous lessons up to that point combined. After class was finished, I was approached with a banner outside of the classroom. It was sitting under a drama rehearsals poster, and it was adjacent to a picture of the swimming team winning the regionals. Written in luminous bold letters, *"BASKETBALL TRIALS, 4 PM NEXT TUESDAY AFTER SCHOOL."* An extended grin ignited on my face on its own accord. I was beyond euphoric.

For the next couple of days, it was all I could think about. In school, at home, while I was sleeping, those basketball trials never departed my memory. I made it imperative to train constantly for it. I woke up early every day from the moment I glimpsed the poster to work on my game. It consisted of me rehearsing my free throws along with my layups. This, as well as every day after school, I would take 2 hours to consummate my shooting form along with a variety of other skill sets that I thought were necessary to not only get into the basketball team but to exceed expectations for the basketball coach.

By the time trials came, I was beyond prepared and ready to display my skill set. The weekend leading up to the trials was only an extension of my preparation. I had repeated everything that I was already accustomed to over the years: all the moves and all the footwork I had developed, and I was ready.

Basketball trials came. This was my opportunity for me to showcase myself and to reveal that I was worthy of joining the team. For all I knew, I didn't think anyone trained to the extent that I had all the years that led up to this point. To my knowledge, I had worked on all my weaknesses and specifically crafted every skill that was acquired for the role to the best of my ability. I knew in my heart before even stepping foot inside that gym that I was the best. I had spent so much time playing basketball that I couldn't register anyone as being better than me or even sharing the same love I had for the sport.

I scanned the room to check who I would be competing against, and it was like my eyes were inciting a scary movie and inviting an unwanted nightmare. I had assumed that all my preparation over the years would have prepared me to showcase my abilities. But I was wrong. As soon as I entered the basketball court, my heart dropped: exiting my whole chest.

There were about 50 attendants, but it felt more like 1,000 to me. Everyone seemed bigger. Everyone seemed stronger. Everyone seemed... better than me. I couldn't register what my eyes were telling me. I had seen these students across the school this whole time, and they never seemed to be more intimidating than now. Maybe I never paid too much attention to them as I would often avoid eye contact with my peers. Perhaps they were always this threatening and I never noticed.

By the time the coach blew the whistle and exclaimed, "Everybody at baseline," my mind was already completely shaken. I had lost all the knowledge that I had of basketball.

There was one individual who stood out and caught my unfocused attention. He wasn't as intimidating as the rest. His frame did not replicate a typical basketball player. He was small and frail. Built almost like an almond. Although his stature would categorize him as insignificant, he seemed to stand out the most to me. As we completed a lay-up drill as a warmup - to which I failed - he introduced himself to me. "My name is Amygdala," he stated as he reached his hand at full length to shake my hand. I hesitated at first as my hands were moist and still shaking uncontrollably from the lay-up drill we had completed. After a few seconds, I accepted his request for physical contact and shook his hand.

"Amygdala?" I responded with confusion.

"Yes, Amygdala," he remarked with a slight chuckle. "But you can call me Dala for short."

I replied quickly with "Okay" so I could end this conversation, but he continued with it when he asked for my name. I stated that my name was "Seraun."

He had noticed that I was tense and anxious within the whole environment, so he stated calmly, "Be patient and trust your preparation." By the time he said those words, the coach blew the whistle for the next drill, and that was the end of our interaction. I know he intended to give me a sense of encouragement, but I was far from saving. No words could help me. It didn't seem like anything could help me at that point. My mind was someplace else: other than basketball.

It was like as we progressed with the drills, I had gotten worse and worse. I was missing layups that I would make with my eyes closed. I was airballing shots that usually resulted in hitting the bottom of the net. I wasn't playing my usual self. I knew I was capable of way more than I was portraying. I was making decisions that would convey I was a novice to the game of basketball. I was committing countless turnovers that I should not have been making. Everything that I was accustomed to was suddenly difficult. It was an unnatural experience. It felt like I was being controlled by fear. My mind wasn't at peace that basketball always offered me. I was consumed with anxiety. The thought of not making the team continued to grow as we progressed, and time was running down. I had set such high expectations of myself that I thought I would have been able to achieve but I did not. It only resulted in a poorer performance. Everyone laughed hysterically and pointed at me judgmentally, at least that is what it felt like.

When the trials were finally over, and they were calling the names of the individuals who had made the team, I already knew I wasn't amongst them. I departed the environment before I embarrassed myself further. I was already disappointed with myself, and I didn't want to hear further disappointment verbally. If I had stayed and listened to all those names being called out it would tear me emotionally into smithereens. Instead, I waited. And waited. I waited until everyone was gone. All the players and the coach.

During the period of my waiting, I reflected on all the mistakes that I made. All the moves I knew I could make. All those decisions that I should've made but didn't. Once this theoretical movie was finished, I went back to the basketball court and did everything I felt I should've done plus more. Out of frustration, I stayed for 3 hours executing all the moves I had failed at portraying. Not knowing this while this was happening, the coach watched me. He watched me for the last 30 minutes pouring out my frustration.

Once I was done and in a full sweat and making puddles every step I took, the coach approached me.

In disbelief, he stated, "What's your name?" I replied, "Seraun" for the second time of the day.

"I am impressed with the skills you've displayed for the short duration I've been watching you. You have displayed high skill for someone your age. I want you to be the captain of the basketball team. Is that okay with you?"

 I replied, "Yes" instantly without hesitation. I was left speechless. I couldn't comprehend what just happened. I was grateful for the opportunity and left as soon as the offer was given before the coach had time to change his mind.

When I got home, I told my parents about what occurred while I was at the trials. I didn't give them the full details, only the parts of which they could acknowledge positively. They told me they were very proud, and that was the end of that interaction.

The first day of practice was something I can never forget. I was an hour early: an unbroken reminder of what took place at the trials was my alarm. I wanted to show the coach that he didn't make a mistake in placing me as captain. I wanted to show him that I took the responsibility seriously. I made sure that all my skills were up to speed and sharpened before the start of practice: going through my usual workout regime.

While I was shooting my free throws, I felt a presence lingering up towards me. It was Dala. Still small and frail from the last time we encountered. In a tone that reflected that he already knew, he asked, "So you made the team?" I responded with a rushing "Yes." I wanted to proceed with my daily routine before practice had started. Dala noticed this and remarked, "You put too much pressure on yourself." I replied impatiently, "I need everything to be perfect." Dala responded, "It's okay not to be perfect; imperfection makes perfection over time." I shrugged off his comments and continued to progress with my routine until I was done. Once that happened, it was time for training to begin.

To say I wasn't nervous would be a lie. I was beyond petrified. It still wasn't to the extent of the emotions I endured during the trials but a similar experience. I didn't know how the team would react to me being there in the first place, let alone me being their captain: their leader. These were going to be my teammates. People I was going to rely on in games and vice versa. I had observed all these professionals and how they helped their teammates excel both individually and as a team.

Once the coach blew the whistle to commence our first training, he introduced me to the team. The coach proudly said, "This is Seraun, your new captain." I had gauged the reaction of all 14 players, and they did not seem impressed. Their faces were filled with confusion and shock like they had seen a ghost. One player commented, "Is this some kind of joke." The coach replied, "No, I was incredibly impressed with the skills he displayed after the trials, not like anything I've seen for a player his age. His fundamentals are sound, and he knows how to play the game the right way."

Despite the words of the coach, doubt filled the

room. They had every reason to, at least for them all I executed to them was my nervousness and my below-average skill set, at least in their eyes. They did not see what my coach was impressed by. It was up to me to execute the arsenal that I had developed over the years. Some of them had already seen the dedication I had displayed towards basketball in school, but all of that was an empty vessel due to my performance at the trials. Not to my knowledge, the team had already made a subconscious agreement. An unspoken alliance with who they assumed would be captain of the team. Ikeji. Ikeji was the best player at the trials by a milestone, so it wasn't a surprise when I found out he made the team. His skill set was mediocre, but it was his physicality that triumphed over everyone on the basketball court. His physical frame was enough to intimidate his opponents. I knew I was better than him, but how was I going to be able to convince my teammates to respect me enough so that I could lead them instead of Ikeji? I knew I had the knowledge to pass on to my teammates, but they wouldn't give me the time to display my intelligence. What is the power of knowledge without the influence to use it?

All these thoughts circulated in my mind as practice proceeded and disrupted my focus on the game. I somehow managed to play worse than I did at the trials. Drill after drill I had gotten progressively worse. Drills that had been ingrained into me somehow were a stranger. I felt like I embarrassed the coach. My teammates couldn't have taken the coach seriously. I had made his words a circus show.

The coach then blew his whistle afterwards to give us a 5-minute break. Momentarily I was saved from embarrassment. I incaved myself amongst my teammates as I didn't want to be seen by them. There was a division between me and my teammates from afar, I didn't feel worthy to be in the same gathering of them even though they were my teammates. While hydrating alone in a corner, Ikeji approached me. "I don't even know how you made the team". The whole team adopted mutual agreement to this statement, as I heard their laughter in the background.

My misery was further exacerbated when the Coach announced that we were going to play a scrimmage. We were told to sort out our teams by ourselves.

Ikeji was of course picked first and it was no surprise that I was picked last. When I was picked it seemed my partners in this scrimmage were disappointed in me playing alongside them. I was determined to prove both my teammates wrong as well as the opposing team that I deserved to be among them.

When the scrimmage started the words of Ikeji echoed both mentally and physically within me: it manifested in the way I played. I let his opinions reconstruct my emotions. The question of whether I was good enough was renounced in my head. As the scrimmage commenced, he was able to worsen my performance. He was also playing far better than me, utilising his strength and vertical ability to exploit our lack of athleticism. He was getting easy fast break layups. He was far quicker than our whole team, he looked like a grown man playing against toddlers.

In comparison to my performance, I was committing aggressive fouls, I was losing the ball, and I was just frustrated in every aspect. To add to my exasperation, I wasn't receiving the ball. They didn't pass to me, nor did they care whether I was open. A lack of passing only initiated me to receive the ball in any way I could. I was diving for loose balls and going for every rebound, both offensively and defensively, putting my body at risk just to have a chance to at least contribute.

Approaching the end of our scrimmage, one of my teammates took a shot and I accurately predicted where the ball was going to land. I positioned myself to receive the ball, however, Ikeji was also in an attempt to get the rebound. We both collided, but ultimately, he received the rebound and made an outlet pass for his team.

Internally I was boiling immensely. I never was able to have my way in anything I did on the court. All my turnovers, my not receiving the ball, and Ikeji outperforming me were an enzyme to my frustration. All I saw was red. I lashed out immediately towards Ikeji and that was all I remembered.

The continuation of this confrontation was recalled to me by Dala, who stated that I clenched my fist at a 45-degree angle and extorted force upon Ikeji's chin. This then resulted in a duel that consisted of multiple punches, kicks, and bruises. We were both immensely hurt but the condition I was left in was far worse than Ikeji.

Dala later came towards me after practice (when I had gained awareness) and highlighted, "The game of basketball is mental as well as physical, if you cannot control what is internal, how can you ever expect to produce externally? Exterior noise in the form of insults and negative comments is only placed to test you: to grade your resilience. If you let one minor comment have agency over you, you have not only failed your team of your talents, but you have failed yourself of your expectations."

Still steamed, I dismissed his comments and went to sit in isolation to calm myself down. Instead of leaving me in isolation, Dala followed me. "Try not to be a slave to your emotions. Don't let your emotions dictate your decisions, it shouldn't have agency over any outcome in your life".

"Why?" I responded.

"Your emotions fluctuate. They are unpredictable and uncertain. They can change within seconds. If you can have authority over your emotions, it will save you from the burden of regret in all aspects of your life".

After this interaction took place, Ikeji and I were banned for a short period from the Basketball team. It gave me a few days to reflect and evaluate my emotions. I had never displayed such anger to someone before it would always be to myself out of frustration. I had built up a bank of wrath and bottled up my frustration that I had nowhere else to store it other than the exchange of my fists. There are simply times in my life when I lose control. I lose stability and recognition of my surroundings. I do not know where I am or what I have done. It's like I'm in a different world, where all forms of vision are red. The name of this world is violence: where temper is the overarching oxygen. Instead of crops and vegetation, there are thorns and spines. Instead of water flowing swiftly like a perfect circuit, there is scorching lava that moves stiffly.

During my time off my coach constantly reminded me of the new responsibilities that came with me being captain. He preached that I should not only lead by example but to understand how to communicate with each teammate. He would say that each teammate has different tendencies and will respond differently based on how you communicate with them. Some teammates you may be harsher with and some you may be more encouraging with he exclaimed. The only way I would be able to execute this would be to develop a relationship with each of my teammates. I had to be able to learn what motivates them, what discourages them and what makes them angry. I needed to know whether they were more driven by team success or individual success. Either would be fine, but it was important to decipher the sole factor on why they joined the basketball team. Did they want to join out of pure love for the game like me? Or was it just to have fun? These were the questions I would try to seek during my interactions with them. I wouldn't ask them these questions directly but rather see how they reacted and manoeuvred during practices.

Even though I comprehended everything my coach advised me to do, executing them was going to be a problem for me. I had all the knowledge and tools to pass on to my teammates, but the struggle was transferring that knowledge to them. My teammates didn't respect me, nor thought I was even good enough to play on the team. Despite my IQ for the game, I always struggled to communicate with people, so how was I going to be able to communicate with my teammates? I was unsure how I was going to be able to appear likeable enough, but I had no other choice but to try.

Our next practice had arrived, and it was a sense of redemption for me. I had to prove not only to my teammates that I belonged to play alongside them, but more to myself that I wasn't a disappointment.

The drills that commenced weren't unfamiliar to me. I seemed to pass through them with ease. However, this did not seem to uplift my spirits, it was the scrimmage that would be the real dictatorship of my emotions.

Upon the coach blowing his whistle to start the scrimmage, my teammates didn't pass me the ball. I assumed their reluctance was based on their already pre-analysis of what I had shown them as well as their allegiance to Ikeji. To me, it was all a misconception of my behaviours and skills, but eventually after a few rebounds and defensive stops, I received the ball a lot more. As my teammates passed me the ball, I was able to hit a few shots. I was more vocal within plays and encouraged my teammates regardless of their faults or successes. However, my dominance lasted short, as the time it took for my teammates to eventually pass me the ball, the scrimmage was over. I was only able to show them a glimpse of the standard I was accustomed to playing at.

After the scrimmage took place, my coach brought me to the side and reiterated to me "You played well but I know you are more capable of what you're portraying. I want you to show the team the same player I saw after the trials. Once you can do that, that's when you will gain the respect that you desire from your teammates."

His words gave me a sense of hope and reassurance, but I still wasn't content with my performance: my expectations were much higher than that. I had a week until the next practice and it gave me time to improve not necessarily skills-wise but rather tactically. I had to come up with ways on how I was going to improve my reputation within the team. I had pictured different scenarios and opportunities on when and where I was going to receive the ball and maximize that chance to portray my abilities. I had a small room for error, being that I didn't receive the ball that much.

Unfortunately, all this work was rendered useless when it came to the next practice and the foreseeable practices after that as well.

The practice where I did play well was a singular star amid thousands. The way I played did not change, but the respect and trust of my teammates stayed constant throughout. They still conveyed emotions of distrust. Their value was rather transferred onto Ikeji. Ikeji's respect was just peculiar. He was able to make a presence on the court that far outreached mine. His likeness was effortless. Everyone on the team naturally gravitated towards him as if he were a magnet. I was the only one repellent to this chemical reaction.

Dala had confided in me once again. "Your viewpoint on yourself is so negative that it reflects onto your teammates."

"What do you mean?" I questioned.

"How you treat yourself reflects how you treat

others. If you respect yourself, others will respect you, if you are kind to yourself, others will be kind towards you. If you show love towards yourself, you will receive love from others. It is all a chain reaction that starts within yourself."

I looked away with a ponderous sigh. "I just want the same respect that my teammates show Ikeji for me."

"Never compare yourself with anyone," Dala responded. "Focus on you. Jealousy breeds hatred over time which is just wasted energy that could be put elsewhere. Instead of envying someone, use whatever they have in their life that you like as a form of motivation to obtain that."

"If I'm able to reach the same level of honour that is shown on Ikeji then I'll be able to be a better captain," I responded.

Dala highlighted, "You should only strive to be a better version of yourself than you were the previous day, any other expectation leaves room for envy, which will always be an unrealistic goal to chase."

"But his life just seems better than mine: on and off

the court. He has everything that I could ever want: teachers like him, his parents don't pressure him to try other hobbies, every aspect of his life is just better."

"Everyone's situation is different," Dala affirmed. "Not everyone's story starts and finishes the same way," he added. "Everyone has a different path and a different journey. You should not feel the need to compare yourself to someone else because you do not know what that person has been through, or what that person has experienced and overcome. You should be grateful for the life you have but not content, always feel the need to strive for more and pursue more."

"How do you expect me to be grateful for the family I have? Ikeji never argues with his parents, and they are not bothered about what he wants to do with his future."

Dala responded frustratingly, "You're missing what you just said. They're not bothered. They don't care whether he succeeds or fails."

"But he still has leniency with them, he's able to do what he wants without them dictating every little thing he does," I argued.

"You are fortunate to have both parents who care deeply about the outcome of your life. You should feel very fortunate with what you have."

"His family… just seems perfect to me," I stated.

"There's no perfect family anywhere: if there is they are just perfect at hiding their imperfections."

"I still wish I had his family," I nagged.

Dala foregrounded, "Family is the only thing in your life that stays consistent: beyond basketball. You can't ask for a new family, nor replace the role they have in your life. Most of the time they have the best interest for you. Nothing will ever love you more than your family. You may bicker and argue, but you will eventually amend everything that is broken. Amendments among your family are a continuous task. It's never finished nor settled, but that's part of what comes with family: an unbreakable chain that binds you for life."

Chapter 4

KINDRED

Over the years I have developed a brotherhood: a relationship that exceeds beyond the basketball court. They are not just my teammates; they are more so my family. Each one of them holds a special place in my heart. The depiction of such an unbreakable bond that I could have never imagined. Our alliance was not limited to the setting of a basketball court, even though that was where we spent most of our time together.

The basketball court was our second home, and they were my roommates. Our rent was the time spent on the basketball court, pushing each other to the limit. Our landlord was our coach who expected the best from us each time we stepped forth on the court. Our payment to him was our effort and in response, he was sheltering us, a setting to express ourselves.

As we spent more and more time together, gradually I started to know them more and revealed sides of myself that I did not even know. They unveiled and unlocked part of me that I was getting to know alongside them. It was the four of us: Me, Ikeji, Elijah and Dillon.

Let's start with Elijah, 'the glue' as we called him. We called him this as he stuck our friendship together. He is the reason why there is still a friendship in the first place. With opinions and views differing amongst us, Elijah made sure to modify any disputes and disagreements we had: the missing piece to our puzzle. He was the counterbalance to any arguments we had, which occurred frequently. He always knew the right things to say that would make each of us just simply stop: stop arguing, stop bickering, just stop being unkind to each other. Whenever our friendship reached the tipping point, he would always secure us to stability, without him our friendship would have crumbled.

In terms of my friendship with Ikeji, it never started as I would have imagined. I never imagined being friends with him, to be honest. We were always in constant battle: at first, initiated on the basketball court. It was based on the underlying fact that I was Captain and Ikeji wanted that role, so he did everything he could to achieve that objective.

We battled on every aspect of the game: who would get the rebound, who would touch the line after finishing a suicide. Suicides was always a constant battle because our positions didn't exclude us from participating in the drill equally. 'Suicides' was a conditioning drill and bared its name because after finishing the drill you felt like death was near. The drill consisted of touching four lines on the basketball court. The first line was the mid-point between the end-line and halfway line, the second line was the halfway line, the third line was the same as the first line but just on the other side of the court, and the last line (if you got that far) would be the ending. All lines were completed once you ran back to the starting position. After an accumulation of all the lines that was one suicide. The coach only expected us to usually do 5 as a warmup, but at the pace me and Ikeji were going, we were exhausted after 2 or 3.

Despite my friendships with Ikeji and Elijah, I was

closest to Dillon. We were integrated. He was a part of my lifestyle. We did everything together: go to school together, be in the same class and sit next to each other. He's the reason why the school was not as boring as it was advertised. I would get in trouble with teachers because of my constant laughing. I never did any of the work: too distracted to even pay attention to what the teacher would be saying. When he wasn't in school for whatever reason, it made going to my different classes a chore as I had no one to talk to. I could have talked to Ikeji and Elijah, but they were never located within communicating distance, I would have had to shout and that would have resulted in me being sent out of class yet again.

Besides, our conversations would never have been on the same magnitude as Me and Dillon's, it wouldn't have flowed the same. With me and Dillon, it was natural: time never moved when we were together. Hours would go by, and we wouldn't even realize. Our interdependence was planted within the stories and laughter shared between us. I would never struggle to make conversation with Dillon, I was at my most natural and most comfortable form.

Naturally, he wasn't always going to be available for me, but I felt like over time he made less effort.

"It feels one-sided," I complained to Dala.

"Never feel the need to chase people if none of your relationships are reciprocated, do not entertain them." "No one ever makes time for me the way I make for them," I argued. "Sometimes people are busy," Dala exclaimed. "They are not always going to be there for you, and you cannot blame them for that. They have their life to live and so do you. You need to learn how to be self-sufficient. You should be your own best friend. You should be able to spend time with yourself and be comfortable in solitude. You should be able to tell yourself anything and not be judgmental towards yourself. When you're able to do that then you can have better relationships with the people around you because you are not relying on them to have quality time, they are only a bonus to your life. They only add extra value towards your life because you are already able to add value to yourself in isolation."

Despite Dala's principles, I didn't listen. I detached myself from Dillon and the rest of my friend group out of spite. However, this did them no harm, the only person I was causing harm to was myself. Their unavailability made me jealous and thinking that they didn't want to be around me anymore. It made me immobile. I built a cage of emotional ferocity and ignored my friends when they reached out to me.

I took that anger into our practice, and it was obvious to even the third party that there wasn't any chemistry anymore. It was clear that something was wrong and as practice advanced it was even more clear.

I had made a pass to Dillon but from his viewpoint, it was too hard. His response to this was passing the ball back to me but with even more extensive force than my pass. I passed the ball back to Dillon, but this wasn't a pass, it was a launch. I didn't throw the ball to pass it to him, I threw it intending to cause harm to him. After I had thrown the ball to Dillon, he stormed to me with rage. We were grappling with each other until we were held away from each other by our other teammates and our coach.

"Do not be so selfish to the point where you let your bad mood transfer onto someone else," Dala said to me while trying to calm me down. "You cannot let your emotions have agency over you because if you do you will regret your decisions in the long run. Whether your emotions are positive or negative try to come into a neutral state of mind before you execute any major decisions. Before you interact with people try to at least be within an emotional state that doesn't transfer negatively unto someone else, that way you will get the most out of that interaction and you will leave a positive influence on that person."

"It's not my fault," I argued.

Dala responded, "Neither of you is wrong but that also does not mean both of you are right. Both individuals mustn't quarrel over their perspectives, they should instead come to level ground and be able to use reason and knowledge to not necessarily comprehend each other, but just accept each other's different opinions as opinions and nothing more than that. At the end of the day, any external opinion should never affect you internally."

After our altercation, I went to Dillon to seek his forgiveness. I told him that I was sorry in the hopes that we could amend what was already broken in our friendship. For some reason, I had the impression that he didn't accept my apology. Things still seemed the same between the two of us and there was still some awkwardness between our interactions.

There's a whirlwind of thoughts when you lose someone you once spent a lot of time with. You start to think about what you could have done differently to amend their departure. You start to ponder how you acted during your interactions. Was I too expressive? Was I too open with that person, or did I not reveal too little about myself? I confessed my worries to Dala.

"What you perceive as something may be completely different from someone else's point of view. Whatever negative impression you think someone else has of you is usually just a portrait of your insecurities."

Chapter 5

ELOQUENCE

The game was set, and everything sparked. All our plays were executed perfectly. Everything the coach said and asked of us was comprehendible and translated into practicality. Players were making cuts at consummate angles where they could receive the ball for a layup. Our defence was sound, collectively retaining steals and constantly making the other team turn the ball over. We were getting every rebound: both offensively and defensively. We were moving the ball well, making sure every pass was crisp. The bench was energetic and showed enthusiasm for every point we scored and every defensive stop we obtained. The referees weren't biased or making decisions that favoured the opposing team. We were winning by a substantial margin. I was having a good game, even to my standard. I was making good passes; I was protecting the ball when defenders were pressing me. I was scoring with ease in different ways: I was getting fast break scores. I was scoring off offensive rebounds. I was scoring off free throws and pick-and-rolls. My touch and shot were feeling better than ever, scoring with high arching shots as well as floaters. Mentally, I was in a good space: when I did miss a shot, I did not overthink it. I was not intimidated by the opposing team, I was locked in. During a timeout, the coach told me that I wasn't going back on defence. I ignored his complaints. We were winning by 30 points up to that point and anything he said would have just been extra noise.

When I was subbed out for my disobedience, Dala had highlighted to me, "Don't let your pride block you from, receiving more knowledge. You're never too smart or intelligent to learn something new. The smartest people are driven by curiosity."

I still ignored Dala and the coach's remarks as we were winning by a lot, and I was also having a good game. I spent the rest of the game rehydrating on the bench and cheering for my teammates. When the game ended, we won by a 42-point margin. That game was only an extension, an extension that ran all the way until the end of our season. From that specific game, our success carried onwards. What I thought was a fluke of a game and would only be a few games, carried on for a few more weeks after that and a few weeks after that as well, until it became normal for us to win by that margin. We adopted a winning culture; the thought of losing did not even cross our minds. The coach's challenge was not whether we needed to win a game, but rather by how much. This was a goal of ours, to exceed the point difference from our previous game. We would win by 50, 60 and at times a 70-point margin, but the coach never let us talk about those games, he didn't want us to get too big-headed and arrogant.

Knowledge of our winning streak started to circulate around the school. Our school never really had much success in athletics, so every win we had was a big deal for them. We were put on announcements in the school, we had big pictures that filled walls of our success on the basketball court. Headteachers shook our hands when we walked past the hall, we were even mentioned in assembly at times. We were asked to stand up and identify ourselves. 15 of us would stand up one by one and our peers and other teachers in the assembly would applaud. Even though I was always reluctant to stand up and identify myself, I always enjoyed this segment in assembly, a segment where I would get recognized, it was a change to the usual proceedings of assembly. It would usually be a singular teacher nagging about our poor collective behaviour, but somehow, I always felt targeted. Whenever a teacher spoke about their concerns on a particular issue, they would glare out at me amongst the hundreds of students in the same place. So, when I was recognized for something good, it was an opportunity to flaunt it to other teachers. Everyone in school gave praise to the basketball team. I had never received such attention like that.

Dala had seen me overjoyed and questioned me. "How do you measure success"? This was the first question he had ever asked me.

I had specifically crafted my response to appear intelligent towards him. "Receiving rewards and being acknowledged for your hard work", I replied. "If you are playing basketball for praise and recognition, then maybe you do not love it as much as you say you do. Whether or not you're acknowledged for your efforts, your hard work should be derived from your self-progression. If you are in a better place than you were the previous day, that's a success. Whether that is mentally, physically, or emotionally".

Dala's vexation didn't move me in any regard. He didn't understand how uncommon the attention was for me even though it was collective praise. I didn't go to practice the next day because I saw no purpose in it. We were just coming off a win and individually I played well. I didn't think there could be anything else we could work on as a team that would help us in games.

"What happened to your work ethic? Dala argued. What happened to your drive? You're getting too complacent. You're letting all the attention and recognition get to your head."

"No, I am not. I have worked so hard to a point where I am playing the best I have ever played."

Dala responded, "You never want to be satisfied, you always want to feel that you could have done a little bit more than you have accomplished for the day. If you stay content, you will never progress. If you have a sense of paranoia about not working hard enough, you will always be willing to improve your output compared to the previous day. You want to be utilizing and maximizing your 24 hours as best as you can, that way you do not have feelings of regret, you will instead feel satisfied when it is all said and done because you will know within yourself that you extracted everything out of life and did all that you could physically do to progress".

"How do you expect me to progress when we are having such a good season?"

"Everything is about improvement," Dala remarked. "How can you be a better son? How can you be a better teammate? But most importantly how can you be a better individual to yourself? You always strive to be a better version of yourself than the previous day".

Despite our collective performance on the basketball court, my reputation around the school remained relatively the same. My isolation only grew deeper. It was like the different comments and opinions kept closing in on me and suffocating me. I had built a reputation: a foundation of uniqueness, a negative kind. I had no control over it either. It didn't matter whether as a team we won or lost. It didn't matter whether I played well or not. Nothing mattered. I was labelled as 'weird' regardless. I wanted to understand how I could portray myself differently to change this, however, Dala had a contrasting opinion.

"You are who you are and that is what makes you an individual. Do not feel the need to change who you are to make others comfortable and to satisfy their wants. You become a victim to yourself when you feel the need to change your behaviours."

My perception differed from my teammates. They didn't receive the same scrutiny I did, more so compliments for their performance on the basketball court. I was an outlier to a group of individuals who were put on a social pedestal. It seemed that I had no reason to associate myself with them. I didn't belong. Dala had confided in me and tried to reassure me with his words.

"Excessive pondering of other people's validation will limit your capability as you're restricting yourself to trust your own capacity. Trust within yourself will allow you to reach a point where other people's opinion of you does not bother you. Your confidence initially should be based on your devotion to the game of Basketball. The fact that you are good at something should give you reassurance of yourself. But as you mature within yourself at the heart of your confidence should be rooted in your love for yourself. And when that time comes that will initiate you to become fearless. They will try to label you as "introverted, `shy" or 'timid,' You cannot get discouraged by these labels; you are only these labels if you allow yourself to be them. All these titles are a reflection of your indifference to them. All that it really entails is their lack of comprehension of your behaviour. There is nothing wrong with being different, we should all be different in fact. Being different shows that you are an individual who is rational and does not require other people's actions to fixate on your own life".

"I just don't understand why my performance on the basketball court isn't mirrored with my life in school. Why is it only me that has to deal with this on the team?"

"It's good to have high expectations of yourself, but unrealistic expectations of yourself where you're comparing yourself to other individuals can be fatal to your mental health."

Chapter 6

TEENAGER

When the season was over, everyone around our school started to pay notice to the basketball team. By the end of the season, seats were packed just to see us play. We kept shocking people with our performance, but they were also celebrative of how successful we were as a team. We were the underdogs coming into the season: no one thought we would even grasp five wins, but we exceeded all expectations. Each of our successes contributed significantly to our team's success. We were able to play beyond our imaginations and achieve the ultimate goal that was set out: to win the league.

With everything being perfect, it came at a detriment: particularly to me. Because we achieved such excellence, I tried to replicate that perfection in every aspect of my life. I set an expectation for my life that mirrored the previous season we had achieved on the basketball court.

Dala would often say to me, "Do not chase happiness, chase experiences. Those experiences may be negative or positive, but you will learn from them regardless."

But his words served no purpose. Empty words. I was so attached and obsessed with living in the past that I lost sight of the present. I wanted to reach a state of perfection that I experienced last season.

The first form of perfection that I tried to fixate on was my perception: changing how people viewed me. I was only going to do this by applying another layer of emotion, an extra layer that people would see. I first began throughout the last stretch of my previous season. I gave an expression, a demeanour on the basketball court. I appeared unfazed and mentally strong throughout any outcome, as it was all I was ever taught. It was drilled into me. I shouldn't reveal my vulnerability to people; it showed weakness, my coach would say. "As an athlete, you're not meant to show mental incapability, or else that can be exploited. They will target you and use that to have agency over you." This did make sense to me; my opponents were never going to be empathetic toward my emotions.

They had every reason and intention to find any type of weapon they could use against me. So, I put on a mask, a psychological resilience mask. I wasn't influenced by any comments or noise while I was playing. This did seem to be successful, but I couldn't put on the mask forever. Off the court, I couldn't achieve the same frontage I performed.

I tried to put on another mask when I was in school, a mask much easier to sustain. I appeared happier, and more vibrant than I was to have more friends. I was ingenuine with my laughter, and I let things that would bother me seem meaningless, all in the pursuit of being accepted. But it was all a lie; a shield, and when people were not looking, I was a completely different person. I was able to deceive everyone apart from me. When I left the basketball court, when I left school, when I left the fake world I created, I was unrecognizable.

At home, I could be myself. I didn't have to hide myself or pretend to be someone else; it was just me and my family. They knew me better than anyone, sometimes even more than myself. They had been to all my games: both bad and good. They had seen me frustrated, angry, and overjoyed, but most importantly, they had seen me, the real me. The me that didn't hide or put on a facade.

"What do you want for dinner?", my mother shouted.

"Lasagne!".

"Alright, come help me."

I then solemnly went downstairs and approached her.

"What's with the frown on your face? You don't have bills to pay", she chuckled.

"Why does it matter whether or not I pay bills?".

"It was only a joke, darling. Don't take it so seriously," she replied.

"It's not like I'm suddenly excluded from distress. I may not have the same responsibilities, but it doesn't mean I dwell in a dystopian world. You don't understand what I go through. I have to put on this emotional outline to be accepted by my peers, and it's draining." "I see," she replied. We then shared a couple of seconds where we just stared at each other. "Son, have you ever heard of the poem *The Undecorated Mask*."

"No." She then went to her room without saying anything and then returned opening a scrunched piece of paper. "This poem helped me a lot while I was growing up":

Upon bird's eye view there is a variety of masks
Some layered with happiness and joy
Others layered with sadness and coy
But all seem to be adopting similar tasks

Imperfection after Imperfection are seasoned over with fabrications
Facial cloaks to cover fears and tears
Violence shielded by passivity
Sorrow veiled with happiness
Scars wrapped around with Immunity
But all seem to hide their inner feelings with illustrations

I am not fooled by their attempts to convey a façade
I see beyond their appearance
Their performance has an expiration date
A time when they will become unrecognizable
A time where eyes are turned
But the fellow who adopts the most genuine trait
Is the Undecorated Mask

A mask that seems to stand out amongst the rest
Plain, Simple, and unexpressed
It doesn't pretend and try to impress
A mask that has no guilt of looking the best

All exteriors are on their journeys to their inevitable cask
Disrupted by delays of perceptions and opinions
But smoother journey is bestowed on the undecorated mask

Masks may receive praise and recognition
And may get applause for their exhibition
But originality belongs to the undecorated mask

They may gather and hide their troubles in their masque
But the one who obtains most peace is the undecorated mask
So, I ask the question, which mask do you wear?

"Who wrote it?" I asked eagerly.

"Come help me make this lasagne."

Once the food was prepared, I stuffed my face and then fell asleep.

The second form of perfection I was trying to amend was the brokenness of my family. I wanted to fix the bond my parents once had for each other. Their bond was the first connection I saw an individual have for another thing; in turn, it helped me recognize the bond I had with a basketball. I needed to repair them. The only way I was going to be successful in doing this would be to isolate myself amongst my friends: they were only going to be a distraction in what I was trying to achieve.

Dala had recognized my self-inflicted detachment from my friends. He appeared to me as usual: unnoticed and discreet.

"What troubles you?"

"Sometimes I hear my parents roar at each other from my room. I feel the depths of my house tremble as my parent's exchange insults and complaints to one another. I put my headphones on to mute their disagreements, but their arguments are ear-piercing."

Dala responded, "It's not your responsibility to amend your parents' issues."

"Yes, it is. I somehow feel like I'm the root of their

verbal violence. I am responsible for their dispute. I always felt a sense of disparity when it came to the family problems me and my friends shared. They have siblings, and I was the only one who did not. I always wished I had an older sibling: a brother preferably. Someone who I could talk to and share my household struggles. My friends had individuals to confide in and relate with each other. They had individuals who understood what they were going through because they too experienced it themselves. I had no one on the other hand. I had no one to utter my trauma to and to share my feelings with. I was yet again isolated in another area of my life, and I had no control over it. I had to deal with this burden all by myself."

"I understand," Dala reiterated. "But you need to understand that life is unapologetic and unforgiving. It does not care about your feelings. It does not care how tired you are. It does not care what you did yesterday or what you plan to do tomorrow. Life is filled with problems. You are never going to run out of problems. You should not expect anything from life; your expectations should be low. Only you can shape your own life.

It is up to you whether you want that life to be positive or negative. You and only you can dictate what life you obtain."

"How is that fair? How am I supposed to deal with all these problems all by myself? I can't keep relying on your advice to satisfy momentary pain."

Dala reiterated, "Your first instinct should not always be to seek advice and counseling; you are a rational being who can make decisions and can decipher what is right or wrong. You have had personal experience, which you should have learned from, that is individual to you and only you. To be honest, only really you can give yourself the best advice because you know what you are feeling and the different encounters that have occurred in your life."

The third form of perfection I attempted to achieve was my social interactions. I wanted to improve how I interacted with different people, especially within my school. It was always a challenge for me. I wasn't good at making new friends: all my friends were in the basketball team. It was a different scenario with them because it was inevitable that I was going to communicate with them. I felt like the friends I did have were only there because I played basketball. Basketball was an extension of my personality trait. I felt like I should have been defined more than just playing basketball. Basketball was what I did but not who I was, and I wanted to show my peers that.

When I got into those interactions, I was unable to express myself. I was mute. In my head, I was able to articulate different scenarios and conversations: a surrounding where I was sociable. But when it came to those interactions being face value it's like my lips are stuck together, and I lose all aspects of creativity when speaking. I overthought all my interactions to the point that when I got into them, I was speechless.

My overthinking became a barrier to my social life. Like with most of my issues, Dala had detected my overwhelmed nature and tried to consolidate me.

"People normally have this negative perception of overthinking; you can overthink positively. People often say, 'don't think, just do,' and although sometimes that is essential, it may not always be the most rational decision to make. You can be critical about your decisions and tune into every detail and scenario that could potentially come out of that and make the best decision logically."

Dala's words couldn't help me during this situation. I had already found an alternative way: a more practical way, a way that would help me speak to people and not have to think about embarrassing myself with what I said. This way made me more confident without even trying to be; it made me funnier and more likeable.

During this time, I developed a habit: a routine almost. I needed an opportunity to express myself creatively during my conversations, so I started drinking alcohol. I started drinking at the end of last season.

It was a party; a party to celebrate our successful season. Everyone in school was invited so naturally, my anxiety levels were immersible. It was held at Ikeji's house at around 5 pm, and I can't remember what time it finished.

Ikeji thought it would be a good idea to take a sip to ease my tension. I was very tense with everything happening around me. I had never been to a party before, nor been around this many people in such a small breathing space, except for assembly, which was mandatory, and we had done it so many times that I was numb to the feeling. This was different, though.

Ikeji had already taken a few sips along with Dillon before he offered to me. Ikeji had obtained the alcohol from his parents' top-secret shelf, so that no kids would be able to get hold of it, but they must not have known of Ikeji's height; they weren't home enough to recognize how tall he was, anyway.

"Take a sip of this," Ikeji stated.

My initial reaction was no; I was smart enough to know that it wasn't something I should be doing. "Just take a sip; it's not that serious." My reaction again was no with Elijah in support this time.

"Leave him, if he doesn't want to drink, he doesn't want to drink," Elijah exclaimed.

But after extensive convincing from Ikeji, and our natural ability to compete, I took a sip. At first, I was fine, but after a while, I felt an unnatural feeling. A dizziness? No, a buzz? I couldn't describe nor depict the feeling, but I enjoyed it. All forms of anxiety and fear seemed to disappear, and

I was a completely different person that night. I was talking to different people with ease, with no hesitation to approach them. This may not sound as if it was a big deal, but to me I was not even able to utter up words to people I was not comfortable around. Now, under this influence, I could be someone else, someone that wasn't me, that person I hated. From this little sip, I was able to experience just a glimpse of what it was like to be a charismatic, confident person. My eagerness to maintain this state I was in grew that night; as hours went by, I took more and more sips.

Elijah was the only one that didn't drink that night, nor any time after that.

My friends claimed to me the next morning everything I did at the party. I was dancing and singing for everyone to see. I exhibited a performance that I was not aware of. I was out of character and extremely expressive to their story. I did not know of this; I only knew how I felt when I took the first sip and everything after that was just blank. I was keen to the idea of me not having anxiety in social interactions, no restrictions holding me back, so I continued drinking.

I started every couple of weeks when me and my teammates would go out; Elijah was excluded from this gathering, of course. We would go to Ikeji's house as it was the only place for us to obtain alcohol. We would go after school or after practice.

But eventually, I did not need my teammates to be around for me to drink; their influence had no power over me, it was more so the alcohol that had the influence.

The same way Ikeji located alcohol was the same way I found it: at the top cupboard in my parents' kitchen. I would drink discreetly and swiftly, as I didn't want to get caught. At first, my drinking was only now and again, but soon it became once a week, and then before I knew it, I was drinking before every interaction I had with people. It was imperative that I drank, or else I couldn't function. If I had gone a day without drinking, I was unidentifiable. It got to a point where I didn't need interactions for me to drink. It was a daily occurrence. I became addicted without even knowing it. I used it as a mechanism for my isolation. My lack of confidence would be aided by alcohol. When I did drink, I felt more alive than I ever could imagine. I was able to talk to anyone without feeling the pressure of embarrassing myself. I was outgoing and funny. I was making more and more friends, and it seemed life was finally going my way…until one night I faced a life-threatening event.

I was drinking erratically as per usual. However, this night was different. I decided to drink more than usual: more than my body could handle. Sporadically, I blacked out. I was rushed to the hospital; met by my two infuriated parents who weren't aware of my drinking.

Alcohol poisoning was what the Doctor exclaimed. The doctors constantly repeated that I should stop drinking, that it wasn't only bad for my basketball, but it was bad for my health.

When all concerned faces departed my hospital room, I had time to myself. I always kept a small bottle in the side of my pocket for emergencies, and I took a sip to relieve my troubles. However, I was wrong to think I was the only one there in the hospital room. Dala was there as well, glaring at me with his judgmental eyes.

"Too much of anything is usually not good for you; even the least harmful thing can become harmful if you abuse its use. You should do things with moderation. The only thing worth overdoing is pursuing your dream because there are no negative outputs from that, only positives."

"Why should I even listen to you?". I argued. "How do you expect me to trust you when I barely know you? You give me all this advice, but none of it seems to even work. Why should I prioritize the words you say above everyone else in my life? I already have enough people in my life trying to advise me on things that are none of their business."

Dala responded, "Not all advice is good advice, and not all advice is bad. Once you realize that advice is based on individual experience, you will be able to interpret your understanding of what they are saying and use your judgment to dictate your next decision."

Shortly after this interaction, I went into therapy. I knew this problem of mine wasn't going to go away by itself, and with the help of some specialists, I was able to gradually stop drinking alcohol.

The fourth form of perfection I aimed to achieve in my life was improving in basketball. I wanted to at least maintain or improve on the performance I displayed last season. Despite my aspiration, I still had some doubts. Questions of how I was going to be able to live up to last season's expectations resided in me. Sometimes I even wonder whether I'm even good at basketball. Am I even good enough to make it pro? Am I on the right trajectory, or am I just wasting my time? I remarked my concerns to Dala once again, and this time his words soothed me and gave me an insight into my blindness.

"Everyone has a gift," his words were, "we all have that one thing that when we execute, we are naturally good at it and it's effortless: a natural talent. And I believe that specific gift should make you feel special and gain a sense of self-fulfillment in the short-term. That self-fulfillment should make you feel confident within yourself. You may get praise for your gift, or it may go unnoticed, but that does not matter. What matters is that you are assured of yourself from within. Overtime you should start to gain your confidence from within and that can only be built through self-love."

"What is self-love, and how do I show it to myself?"

"By building knowledge of yourself. The only way to show appreciation to yourself is to know who you're appreciating. You're the only one with this entity, so it's up to you to know that entity to the best of your ability."

"How can I learn about something that I think so negatively of?" I responded.

"You cannot be kind to people without being kind to yourself: self-appreciation is a catalyst for a multitude of beneficial aspects in your life. It takes time but eventually you'll get there."

"I need to be able to boost my self-confidence as quickly as possible," I replied.

Dala remarked, "Confidence is not something measured, it is something that builds over time and the growth you take individually. It is a continuation of putting yourself in uncomfortable situations and maneuvering between them. It is overcoming the barriers of self-doubt."

Chapter 7

BLOCKAGE

The fourth quarter had just started, and we were gaining momentum. We were trailing by 4 points, but we were making a rapid comeback. Our hopes were still high. The opposing team was quite skilled as they were leading the game for the first three quarters, but we were not worried, they were nothing compared to our team when we were playing at our full capacity: no team was.

I was having a good game, to say the least, scoring 28 points entering the last stretch of the game. I knew it was my responsibility to take over and lead my team to victory: it was not new to me. Countless times we were put in this same situation, and I was able to will our team to victory. This time was no different, at least that was what I thought. I had just gotten a steal and I was on a fastbreak. In my mind, I was just going to get a simple lay-up and we would only be down by 2 points on the scoreboard: the opposing team and this particular player that was behind me had other plans: plans to foul me.

As I extended my right arm to convert a layup I was met by an opposing player. He jumped into me, and we collided. By the angle at which the opposing player jumped, it did not seem he had the intention to block my attempt to score. The moment we collided, I already knew that something was wrong. I had landed on the side of my ankle, and I was instantly struck with unendurable pain. I was instantly paralyzed. Stagnant. I made a scream that was heard by everyone on the basketball court. My teammates and my Coach rushed towards me, and I was assisted off the court by the shoulders of my two teammates and hurried to the hospital. The only feeling I felt was anguish. I never really considered how long my recovery would take, so I was utterly shocked to learn that it would take six months for me to fully heal.

When I was injured, it seemed everything switched. The people and 'supporters' around me had lost all faith and belief in me. Their uncertainty had transferred into self-doubt. Negative thoughts circulated in my head. Thoughts of whether I was going to make it. Thoughts of whether I was even going to be able to play Basketball. These thoughts were not only internal, as the words of my father also increased in volume in my mind. "You need to think of another career choice: a more realistic one". "There are too many factors that can hinder you from playing." These comments along with my self-doubt dwelled within me: dictating my mind.

Weeks had gone by, and I decided to go to training, not to play, but to still be around the game. I still wanted to be around the game and support my teammates as well. But it was very difficult for me to watch my teammates play while I was on the sideline. Every part of my body urged me to play on the court alongside them, but I couldn't do so. After practice was over and my misery was put to a momentary end, we had to rush over to class as we were running late. Despite still making class on time, the teacher still made known our arrival to the whole class as we were the only students not seated.

"Class, we will be approaching our final year in the next couple of months so you must make plans post-school".

The teacher then proceeded to hand out to each of

our desks an A4 piece of paper where we wrote what school we were going to be enrolling in based on the grades we averaged over the years. We were constantly made aware of our grades, and I was never really bothered with my results. Cs and Ds were the continuous lyrics to my depressing song titled 'Education'. The chorus of this song was the daily exclamation of my teachers shouting 'focus' and 'pay attention'. I did just well enough to get by, but I never really put 100% into school, incomparable to the amount I put into Basketball. My perspective of school never fluctuated from the time I started. My thought was that you attend school to find out what career path you want to pursue, but I was quite certain of that at a tender age. I wasn't a lazy student, but rather aware of what I wanted to do for the rest of my life, and I prioritized most of my time to that. Nothing else seemed more valuable to me.

The other option seen on the piece of paper our teacher gave us was whether we were going into training for a specific job that we wanted. This option was encouraged to me by a variety of teachers due to my mediocre grades, but with neither of the options on the paper being basketball, I left it blank. I wasn't doing this out of spite but rather my inability to confide in aspirational limitations placed on me by my teacher.

Noticing this, my teacher told me to stand up while showing my piece of paper to the whole class. "This is what laziness looks like, someone with no ambition." I remained silent during this as I didn't want to cause any more disputes. This seemed to only make the teacher more enraged.

She questioned, "Why are you so stubborn?"

I finally unveiled my silence and responded, "I'm not, I want to be a professional basketball player."

"How many times do I have to tell you Seraun? You won't make it as a professional basketball player. Shouldn't your injury be enough for you to understand that?"

My face remained unmoved. I sat down afterwards and remained silent for the rest of the lesson, trying not to bring attention to myself.

After class, Dala approached me. "You can't get discouraged after one little setback; you need to welcome it as an opportunity to grow. They're your biggest teacher and will nurture you to achieve your end goal."

"How am I supposed to remain unbothered, when everyone is installing doubt into my mind?" "Just because your dream doesn't meet their expectations of reality, it doesn't mean it's not achievable to you."

I took a deep breath and sighed.

"Your dream is personalized to you and only you. It's your job to nurture it and guard it because it's precious. Trust the preparation you have put in and let reality unfold for itself. Your decisions may not always necessarily coincide with the people that are around you, but that is okay, they don't see your dreams: they are physically incapable of it.

My mother had also seen me unresponsive to our usual dialogue which consisted of me explaining how my day went and whether or not I was hungry. I was emotionally uninvested to follow these conventions. Naturally, I wanted to stay in isolation, but my mother wouldn't let me. She was already aware of the comments my teachers and my father had made towards me. She knew how vulnerable I was to words.

My mother exclaimed to me curiously- "What do you love so much about basketball?"

"Everything" I responded. "I love the anticipation you have deep in your stomach before a game. I love how everything just changes when you start playing. Nothing else matters. I love the creativity it brings, and how you're able to react to different scenarios in your head and manipulate the game. I love the diversity it brings: every player brings something different, something new. You can never find a carbon copy of the same player. I love the attention to detail it requires. I love the cuts and the angles. The sound the net makes when you swish the shot. The silent suspense you have before shooting free throws. The squeaky sound your shoes make when you stop in acceleration. Basketball is a form of expression for me: a way to voice out my emotions in places I felt were silenced: a paintbrush almost where I get to add to a developing picture. It's a never-ending love: a love that grows each day as I learn something new. I will probably never love anything like it".

My mother responded heart-warmingly- "It's a

great feeling when you find that thing that you love deeply. It's indescribable. You must protect it and nurture it with all your heart because it's valuable. You have to be stubborn almost when it comes to chasing your dreams. People may come across your life and try to discourage you from chasing your dream, but don't let their doubt hinder you from setting out what you're meant to do in your life."

I didn't understand why my dad didn't show the same compassion and understanding. He would reveal total contrast. He would often use the line "You have a better chance of winning the lottery than going pro." My reaction towards this did offer me a sense of resentment towards my dad for not believing in me, but I was stubborn enough to ignore his claims, not because I was so certain that I would attain my dream, but rather because the love I had for this sport outweighed any opinion he could have had. Perhaps, it was ignorant to believe that my dad would believe in the same dream I have been constantly imagining and putting into practicality. He didn't share the same love I had. He didn't see the same dreams I did. His lack of belief fueled me even more and gave me the motivation to prove him wrong.

Although I did have this stubbornness, I can't deny the thought of uncertainty did enter my mind. It also didn't help me to see my teammates flourish on the basketball court. With my absence, my teammates were scoring a lot more. Now that my minutes of playing were occupied, players who would usually be on the bench started playing more. Perhaps a positive came from this as they were able to display themselves and they may not have had that chance If I was still playing.

Ikeji took over in my absence. Now that I wasn't playing, he didn't have someone that would score more than him and outplay him. I wouldn't be there to challenge him, not that he wasn't being challenged within the team, but it wasn't to the same extent. Our duel was what made us win by a considerable margin, us trying to outscore each other was what made our team have 20-to-30-point leading games. But that was now over, and it was clear who was the best player on the team. His outperformance would now be singled out, finally adopting the spotlight and he took advantage. He scored more, rebounded more, assisted more, and his overall average improved.

With his performance, other coaches from professional teams started to take notice. They were watching him flourish on the court and started sending him letters: offering him a place on their team once he finished school. It became a bidding war for these teams, and Ikeji had all the power to choose wherever he wanted to go.

It was not like he didn't deserve it, he did, I just wanted to be in the same position. I was happy for him, but I was just disappointed in myself that I wasn't receiving the same letters and recognition. I felt useless.

Dala made it imperative, "You should not ever feel that you are not enough. You are more than enough. Try not to change who you are to satisfy someone else's needs. You may change as a person over time, but that should not be influenced based on other people's perceptions of you. People should accept who you are as a person and all your negative and positive traits and if they do not you should not be involved in that situation."

It got to a point where I started to think of other

career choices: ones that would make me the most money. Dala convinced me that no wage or any amount of money could ever fulfil the joy of doing what I loved.

He stated, "If you love what you do and you have a passion for it, you wouldn't mind sacrificing your time and money because you won't feel like you've lost anything.

"There is no guarantee of success," I argued.

"Success is inevitable when you love what you do."

"But what if I fail?" I questioned.

"What if you don't? What if you exceed past any predictions, you could have ever imagined?"

From that point onwards I went into rehab in hopes of coming back at 100%. I had fractured my ankle and my recovery was indefinite. The Doctors said I may never come back to even play basketball and the uncertainty was what gave me worry. I was put in a cast for a couple of months, unable to do most simple things: I couldn't walk up or down the stairs, and I wasn't able to go to the kitchen at will to get food. I relied on the assistance of my parents to do most things: they ensured that everything was within arm's length of my reach: I was immobilized. The hardest part of this period was when my parents left. I had no one to help me get things, I couldn't walk to get the remote, I couldn't turn off the lights when I wanted, I couldn't open and close doors but most importantly I couldn't play basketball.

A couple of weeks from this, I was able to only stand on two feet, not for long though and the pain was still too much. It was a slow progression, but still some progression. I had to cling to the smallest hope of my recovery; it was the only thing that incentivized me to get better. The hardest part of this was watching all my games on the bench. I didn't like the feeling of not contributing to my team. I was simply on the sideline, making empty noises of encouragement, but it made no difference whether I was there or not. For the first time, I wasn't contributing to my team's success. We were winning, but it did not feel as good as I wasn't physically involved, you could call it selfish, but I wanted to be the reason why my team was winning.

A couple of weeks from me being able to stand on my own two feet, I was able to stand for a bit longer, and gradually progressed to walking. The exercises that were given to me by my doctor were working but they couldn't have been more boring. The exercises were made to re-strengthen my ankle, they were monotonous and strenuous. It felt like I wasn't making any progress.

During this process, Dala highlighted to me that "Patience is key, the best things in life take time to develop."

Months passed I was only able to set foot on a basketball court. I couldn't execute the moves I'd been doing for years. They weren't moving at the same pace I was used to. They weren't as sharp. I tried to persevere, but I was losing hope daily.

"Put small steps forward and eventually you would have climbed Mount Everest." Consistency over quantity. This will enable you to reach your goal. Enjoy the journey. Enjoy every little victory and every little setback that comes your way as within those times you will build mental toughness and start to learn more about yourself. You will start to see how resilient you are and how you are more than capable than you could have ever imagined. The most tangible skill that separates you from the rest is having constant reassurance in your ability even when times may be tricky, and you have lost all hope," Dala reiterated to me.

Chapter 8

ADMIRAL

I was 18 when my father died in a car crash. When I heard the news, I initially rejected the accusation. I thought it was some kind of joke placed on me. But when I realized that it wasn't a form of joke and it was reality: my reality, I felt a sharp piercing pain in the middle of my stomach. A multitude of sensories and emotions hit me like a crashing wave. The first emotion I experienced was regret. It didn't sit well with me how we departed from each other. Our last moments together were spent arguing. Like most of our disagreements, it stemmed from my stubbornness to confide in his aspirational expectations.

"Why can't you just listen to me for once in your life?". "It's my life to live".

"So stubborn, too blind to see the reality of the situation", he remarked.

"Why are you against me playing basketball?".

"There's no stability in it". "What if you get injured again? And can never play? What will you do then?".

I was unresponsive and unmoved for some time and then I quickly added, "That won't happen".

"You don't know that", my father stated. "Be realistic", he continued.

"There's nothing else I would rather do", I replied.

"Sometimes you have to look beyond what you want and be responsible", he recommended.

"I'll prove you wrong. I'll show you. I'm not going to end up like you". I then stormed out of the house, slamming the door with immense force.

Those were the last words I ever spoke to him. Not a day goes past where I don't desire this scenario to be different: a more positive one: "I understand son, I am in full support". "I believe in you and trust whatever path you decide to venture on, you will be successful". "Thank you", I would have replied. Then we would hug and say that we loved each other. That's how I imagined it would end, how he'd leave my life: not on the terms that actually occurred, I try not to think of it that way.

The initial regret I felt was soon aided by anger. I felt angry that it was me that had to go through this. All the things that I've been through and overcome. Why was it me? What had I done to receive such heartache? I was both heavy and empty inside. I would never be able to fill the void of a fatherly figure in my life. I felt like a burden had been placed on me yet again but this one wasn't going to leave. I wasn't going to depart from this, and it felt like I had to deal with it all alone. A whirlwind of anger never drifted away from my emotions, I felt angry at the reckless driver that caused this. I felt angry at myself mainly, for how I treated my father, I wasn't the best child to him. I could have been a better son, a more obedient one, one that listened and wasn't disrespectful. I often acted out of anger towards him as I felt that the one individual that should show support to me, should come from him. I resented the fact that he didn't believe or support me. I knew that in his own eyes, he was seeking what was best for me, but what was best for me was basketball, that is what he didn't realize, what he won't ever realize.

After this, I stayed in my room, curling myself in a corner. I did not want to see anyone, nor speak to anyone. I refrained from telling my friends of my father's death at first, but my mother had notified the school of my absence. My friends made efforts to console me, but I pushed them away. I appreciated their concern, but I wanted to be in solitude. I kept hearing the phrase that I needed to find ways to "move on" as if his death was a form of momentary event that I am supposed to deviate from. I rejected such commands. I made it imperative that my father would stay with me. When I do speak of him, I won't be talking in the past tense, he is still very much present in my life. He lives within me, a part of me that I will carry until my time comes.

Though at times we may have had disagreements, he was still very much present in my life and shaped me to become the person I am. Though I am not perfect now, the individual I am would have changed without the presence of him. His presence affected me both positively and negatively.

As a child, I always felt the need to prove myself: a

constant verification that I always looked for. If I were able to show him that I was able to play basketball, then maybe that would alter his doubts about me pursuing it as a career. Perhaps the disapproval of my father in everything I did made me such a perfectionist. I strived to reach his acceptance to the point that when I didn't reach it, I internalized his disappointment into myself. It was why I was never able to be fully satisfied with the work I did. I was never able to appreciate any of my milestones because I never felt good enough and that started with the condemnation of my father.

For the next couple of weeks after my father's death, I didn't go to training. The thought of being around people other than my mother was unbearable. There were times when I saw children with their fathers, and I couldn't help but feel resentment towards them. I was jealous. I wasn't going to able to experience what they experienced. Thus, I expressed my grief the only way I knew how: through the basketball court. For those couple of hours of the day, I was able to forget about everything and put my mind elsewhere. But when I left the basketball court all my emotions came back. My father still wasn't with me, and I was still empty inside. I was sleepless at night. I simply just wasn't myself.

Dala approached me like he always would, "What makes you sad?'

"My... my... my."

"Your father?".

"Yes".

"What happened?', Dala questioned. I sobbed uncontrollably. "I understand", Dala reiterated.

"What is even the point?".

"What?", Dala questioned.

"Life". "What is even the point if we all just go away?"

'There's beauty in the uncertainty" Dala stated. "Without life, there isn't death, they're interdependent". I turned away in disagreement as I scraped a tear from my plumbed face. "If you look at it from that perspective then you can appreciate the scarcity that comes with it." "I just regret how everything happened, how everything was left". "You can't control the past its only there for you to learn."

"How do you expect me to learn from this?".

"By appreciating the value of something. You don't realize how valuable something is until you lose it", Dala said.

A couple of days went by after my interaction with Dala, and I was in no better shape. I was both exhausted and restless. There was only one person who I knew shared the same feelings as I did, possibly even worse: my mother. She had lost her husband, her partner in raising me. She stayed strong as best as she could for me, but I knew she was broken inside. She highlighted that the individuals we lose in our lives are in a better place: a place full of tranquillity and away from this corrupted world. She also encouraged me to laugh during this time. I was initially confused by her demands, but she expressed that it would be medicinal for me.

"Laughter is the most efficient and practical way to bring positivity to your life", she made known.

This did help. I searched for laughter among my

friends. I could trust that their company would uplift my spirits as well as give me the closure I needed to fill the void of loneliness I had. I knew my feeling wasn't something that would be easily amendable or necessarily something that I could heal from, but it was a start.

It had been months since my father's passing, and a lot had changed. My father was buried, and a lot of family and friends were in attendance to support him. The service wasn't too long but I cried throughout it all. I cried so much that every step I took was filled with puddles. The funeral service consisted of a hymn that was led by my aunt who sang beautifully. Her voice was like an elegant dove, flying gracefully along the soft clouds and majestically crossing the sky. This was then accompanied by a eulogy, read by my grandmother, it was heart-warming and touched the hearts of everyone that attended.

It was then supported by a speech made by my mother, brief but soul-provoking. She spoke from her heart, and it was evident. This may have been the hardest segment of the entire funeral; I am not sure how she was able to deliver such a message without tearing up.

After everyone felt my mother's speech, we were then queued with my father's playlist. It was all the jazz music he and my mother would listen to when they were younger. After all of this occurred, I noticed individuals from afar: sitting in the back. All of my friends came to support me, all of them came to consolidate me and my mother. Ikeji, Elijah, and Dillon. A piece of my heart was filled when I saw my friends, along with people from a variety of different backgrounds, all gathered for one person: one person who had a profound effect on their lives. I was unaware of the ripple effect my dad had on so many people before he passed away.

A couple of days after my father's burial, I received a letter.

Dear Seraunin,

This letter identifies you as a top prospect for the Reves Basketball Team. After evaluating numerous athletes from around the country, you have been singled out. Members of our scouting team have been monitoring your performance throughout your previous season and as a team, we have been impressed.

Your distribution of athletic ability, leadership and character on the basketball court is unique. Your decision-making on the floor is unmatched: a type of intellect that would fit perfectly on our roster.

 As a team, we would like to invite you to a trial for our team to see how you compare with some of our players. Trials will take place on April 4th from 11 am to 1 pm.

 There will be more details available to you on negotiating contracts after you have progressed from the trial phase. I look forward to seeing you.

Yours sincerely,

Coach David

Reves Basketball Team

Upon first glance at the letter, my first reaction was to reveal it to my mother. I felt impelled to share my joy with someone that I felt understood the severity of what was happening. That letter was the first form of good news that we both received in the past couple of months. We were both speechless as well as overwhelmed. We didn't know how to react. We didn't speak words to each other but we both understood our inner feeling. Everything that I had strived and hoped for since the age of 2, was arm-reach away.

I attended the trials weeks later with the memories of my dad on my right shoulder and a reminder of my mum on my left. Neither of these weights was heavy however, I had carried a far greater burden these last months.

When I entered the basketball court, there were 14 players, and I examined each of them while they were warming up. Each player adopted a unique strength that was superior to the next player I saw. One player was a unique shooter, far exceeding my own ability. He drained every shot he took with range, speed, accuracy, and flawlessness. Each shot he took touched the bottom of the net and everyone's reaction towards the matter looked like it was a usual occurrence.

Another player illustrated a unique defensive ability when playing another 1vs1. The opposing player seemed to struggle to get past him, even though the moves he distributed were far sharper and quicker than what I could ever execute. His capability to recover as well as his lateral quickness was something I had never seen.

Player after player I witnessed a different skill that each of them had mastered over years of practice, but there was one thing I didn't see. I couldn't see a single player that had an accumulation of all these skills. If one player was an outstanding passer, it was his shooting that was his weakness. If another was a remarkable defender, it was his ability to handle the basketball under pressure that limited his performance. Each player was flawed with at least one thing, and this gave me the extra confidence I needed to display my skillset further.

Each drill I was given was required to display my weaknesses, but I was already accustomed to doing that from the moment I could touch a basketball. I excelled with each objective that was given to me and I only clarified the decision of the Coach.

When my examination was over, I was brought into the Coach's office.

"I am impressed with what you displayed today".

"Thank you".

"We would be happy for you to join our team if that is okay with you".

"It would be an honour", I quickly replied.

"Perfect". He then proceeded to slide across the desk a contract along with a pen.

I signed it and a whirlwind of emotions hit me. I was of course proud, but also felt sorrow. My father was never going to be able to see me play professionally. I couldn't show my dad that I finally did it. I finally accomplished everything that I said I was going to do.

A couple weeks after that would be my first match for the team:

Everyone waits stagnant, trembling with fear. Our hearts were racing faster beyond imagination. Moving rapidly by the minute. Each minute getting worse and worse. Apprehensive. Bodies were trickling down with sweat like melted ice. Our palms were drenched. Our Knees were weak. We were almost possessed; unaware of the dedication it took to reach this very point. Almost reaching the finish line but the last hurdle was to obtain the right mentality.

The locker room was being emptied one by one as we were being led out. As more players were leaving the more the roars portrayed grew much with it. Never-ending echoes fill contagiously. From every corner of that building, screeches made themselves known. The chants engulfed me, completely capturing my entire body. Agitated. Unable to function at a mentally stable level. The growling from fans was like a loose bull. They were shouting vigorously to support their favoured team. Ominous noise filled our brains as each of us jogged evenly into the arena. In the eyes of a third party, we are just a moving mass trying to fulfil our day-to-day duties, but in these parts, we are deities representing the people of our city. As we approached, we saw flashes of brightness in various colours. It was quite difficult to explain the ranges of colours due to the quantity but nevertheless, it was vibrant and dynamic. Energetic but still aggressive. It was a type of brightness that beamed through your retinas, closing them sharply with fear of going blind: a type of brightness that had a rivalry with the sun. Despite this brightness, I still felt darkness inside.

Coincidentally darkness filled the building. Darkness came like the thick velvet curtains of a theatre. Silence filled the building, as it was time for the players to be called out onto the court. I heard my name being called out and I knew it was what I had been waiting for all my life. My heart began to drop even lower as I heard more and more names being mentioned.

Countless hours were spent on this very moment, and it finally arrived. "Now from the United Kingdom, at guard who stands at six foot two, Seraunin."

The ball is being thrown off to tip off and the game starts…

Chapter 9

LETTER 1

Dear Basketball,

I have no regrets. Everything in my life that has led up to this very moment occurred purposefully. Right now, I am reaping the benefits of the labour I have put countless hours in. Fearlessness, Persistence and Dedication are the words that were the motor to my journey called life. I consider myself extremely fortunate to have a wife and children who continue to support me in everything I do. There is no other way for me to express my gratitude than by simply saying thank you, and not just to you, but to everyone in my life who has had an impact on me in some way; without them, I am not sure where I would be. I'd like to thank Dala in particular because he was an anchor for me when I was at my lowest point. He assisted me in seeing things from a different perspective than I was used to. He taught me that the journey is more important than the outcome: helping me to see the beauty of progression and not always being focused on the end goal. I now realise that the results do not necessarily matter as long as I am able to dictate everything that I can control and put my all into something, which is far greater than any accomplishment I could ever wish for.

Inner victories allowed me to truly learn more about myself and realise that I am capable of far more than my mind tries to limit. Dala's advice has helped me understand the concept of failure. Through all my experiences, I've realised that there is no such thing as failure: it's a figment of imagination used to motivate me to work even harder. It gives the extra push when hope is lost. It leads through difficult times. Failure creates a thirst for success and a hunger for victory. Failure breeds innovation. Failure saved my life. Dala was able to help me see that. After all these years I never was able to contact Dala. I constantly tried to find him, but I never had any luck. As things improved for me, he simply faded away over time. His advice is constantly implemented to this day.

I now use my time doing other things now. Compared to when I was younger, my priorities have changed. Back then, I was a lot more selfish. I was only concentrated on the progression within myself, and I often neglected the emotions and feelings of the individuals around me. Now I am fixated on how I can influence the generation after me. How can they learn from the mistakes I made when I was younger to ensure they do not make the same ones I did? How can they focus on their dream? It may not be a career in basketball like me but ensuring that they adopt the tools of discipline and resilience to make their own path through life and follow their own passion.

I believe my outlook on life has matured. Before, I would ask myself When will my time come? How will I be able to succeed? What do I need to shape in my life to reflect success? Although those were important questions at the time, they were single-minded filled with relentless ambition that can sometimes be harmful. The questions I ask myself now are: How can I be a better father to my kids?

Am I being a role model for them? What can I do to make sure my kids have a better future than I did?

I'm not worried that my children will make the same mistakes I did, I trust that they will see what I did wrong and learn from that. As a father, I am constantly adjusting to the new experience. It's teaching me patience and empathy. I try to pass on some of the practical lessons my parents taught me to my children. I am going to be more open-minded about what my children want to do in the future.

My daughter Dayla is four now, she was named after Dala. She symbolises so much in my life. She is more outgoing than I used to be: a polar opposite of my former self. She adopts this fearlessness in her, an unnatural kind. She does not care about exterior opinions nor should she. She is a light that shines in the darkest of rooms. I am trying to instil in her to never accept anything but greatness. It may be difficult to achieve, and a lot of pressure is put on her, but I believe it's the only way for her to have a truly meaningful life. I want her to be self-sufficient and not rely on others to do things she can do herself.

She is already portraying such characteristics. She knows what she wants and knows what she likes and what she doesn't like. I rarely have to entertain her, she occupies her own time, without me or her mother having to do anything. She has taken an interest in writing, I never persuaded her or leaned her to it, she found it herself. She ventures all forms of writing: poems, short stories, in her diary etc. My favourite moments are when she reads me out her poems, she is very talented with the way she can manipulate words to suit what she is trying to convey. I encourage her to expand on her curiosity for writing: it's the only way for her love to grow more deeply.

Her talent for writing shocks me perpetually, it was like she was born for it. My son Ivan is only two years younger than Dayla; he hasn't found that very thing to pursue, but that's okay. In a way, I think it's good he hasn't found that very thing yet: it gives him the opportunity to explore a variety of things. He is at that age where there is absolutely no pressure for him, I would rather it happen organically. I don't want him to feel rushed and make it imperative to find it. That's the beauty of it, why it is so pure, you never know when you will find it but when you do it changes your life. I tell my children that once they find their passion: a passion that leaves them sleepless and addicted, it's one of the most rewarding things in life.

My outlook on school has also changed, I know now that it was not necessarily needed for me in terms of directing my career path (I had determined that as soon as I was able to formulate thoughts) but it was needed in terms of developing my social skills and exchanging social conversations. It helped me gauge people's emotions. I always struggled with understanding people. They were puzzles I could not piece together. Basketball was the only thing I could understand at the time. It was not something that I had to predict or to interpret its emotions. It never stopped communicating with me because it was angry at me or had a problem with something I did or said, it comforted me. School helped me to see why people acted in a certain way. It showed me how important communication is. School has given me a variety of events which put me in a position where I became a better person. I am better at comprehending human tendencies because of it.

The lessons my mother taught me I am still able to use. "Everything in life always involves risks: you go to school there is risk, you take the bus or train there is risk, so you might as well take the risk of pursuing your dream". I believe this was single-handedly the most important lesson that I could ever carry on my shoulders.

In retrospect, I see things differently now. My goals in life are not the same now. My priorities are much deeper than just basketball. What matters most to me now is the memories I build. The memories I build with my family, the memories I build with my friends and my players. These are what matter most to me now because they are all that I can carry with me as I get older and older.

Thank you for everything,

Yours Sincerely,

Seraunin

Chapter 10

LETTER 2

Dear Basketball,

You have failed me. I gave you all my time and nothing came out of it. Fruitless. Basketball was an outlet I used to cast my emotions, though those emotions varied, it was the consistency that I fell in love with. Even when situations within basketball differed, the core principles never changed. It was always me and you and everything outside of that for that duration of time did not matter. For that allocated time spent with each other, I was at peace momentarily. Perhaps I was addicted to escaping reality and that may have been why I spent so much time with you. Because I was so fixated on escaping reality, I often tucked away and hid my emotions, thinking that they would suddenly go away and drift someplace else, but they did not. All it did was grow bigger and bigger until it was uncontainable and led to emotional outbreaks that were often difficult for me to explain.

I always expected the worst out of every situation: I expected that I would fail at basketball, and I expected that no one would love me as much as they claimed. I expected that I would never grow as an individual and always be a shell of myself. The only positive thing that could ever come out of this was that I was never disappointed. I was never disappointed in people because I expected the worst in them. I was never disappointed when I did not play professionally in basketball because I had already pictured the scenario countlessly. All these things that I prevented in my life, but at what cost? Was it worth discarding possible relationships that could have flourished? Was it worth never reaching my full potential? If I had seen things more from a positive outlook, then potentially my life would not have turned out the way it did.

I neglected so many relationships because I was so driven by success. Seeking praise hindered so many relationships that I could have had. Was it even worth it in the end? Was I even good enough? What is even the point of pushing yourself if nothing ever comes out of it: only disappointment and regret? Maybe I should have spent more time with my peers. My self-inflicted isolation was more of a detriment to me. I let the comfortability of my isolation guard me from a better life. I always felt like I could've achieved more in my life: like I had a greater purpose than this, one that could've been far greater than I could've imagined. Perhaps if I could've achieved more in my life if I didn't let the thoughts of others affect me. I became a failure because that was all I ever thought about. I was paralysed by fear. The fear of failure. I let the fear of failure dictate my decisions and it restricted my potential. I projected a lot of my fears onto other people without taking any accountability. I assumed that people thought the worst of me, so I shielded myself from interacting with them. I would judge people before I even met them because internally, I judged myself. I was not able to look at myself in the mirror. I was not able to learn how to be comfortable around my own skin and that reflected on all my damaged relationships. I was not able to love myself, so I was incapable of exerting that onto others.

One of the biggest fears that affected me for my whole life was that the efforts I put in were not reciprocated in my accomplishments and gratitude: afraid that if I put everything into basketball and I was to come out unsuccessful, then I would have been a failure of a person. I put so much pressure on being successful that I overlooked what made me fall in love with this sport and what initially grew my interest in it at such an early age.

But in retrospect all my fears were pointless, and a waste of time, I wish I had known that at a younger age, perhaps the outcome of my life may have differed, maybe I would have been able to play professionally, or maybe I could have had a wife and a family, maybe I could have had the life I always wanted...

Thank you for nothing,

Yours Sincerely,

Seraunin

Printed in Great Britain
by Amazon